Captains of industry, widows and orphans, the naïve and the scoundrelly—she has been their champion, and she has seen the darkest places of the heart. These stories explore those dark places and the transformative power of adversity, for good and bad. They are also about the pull of blood, the sinew of old love, and about courage and healing. For those who labour at the law, there will be many I have been there moments. For those who don't, this collection gives a front row seat onto the field of battle.

—**Wailan Low**, Superior Court Judge, Ontario

There are lessons here, about what matters and what lasts, but they are not tacked on at the end of the story, they emerge slowly and arrive as our own discoveries about what it means to be human, in this time, in this place.

—**George Amabile**, internationally acclaimed, award-winning poet

Each story chimes with a grace note. Never has the genre of legal drama weaved gender, culture, heritage, despair and the mysteries of the soul. Great insight and just beautiful writing!

—**Jerry Ciccoritti**, Film Director
The Many Trials of One Jane Doe

I loved Darlene Madott's passion and insight. Only someone who has spent a lifetime in the legal trenches could write stories and characters so original and compelling.

—**Bernard Zukerman**, Producer CBC's reboot of *Street Legal*

Essential Prose Series 203

Guernica Editions Inc. acknowledges the support of the Canada Council for the Arts and the Ontario Arts Council. The Ontario Arts Council is an agency of the Government of Ontario.

We acknowledge the financial support of the Government of Canada.

Winners and Losers
Tales of Life, Law, Love and Loss

DARLENE MADOTT

**GUERNICA
EDITIONS**
TORONTO • CHICAGO • BUFFALO • LANCASTER (U.K.)
2023

Guernica Founder: Antonio D'Alfonso

Michael Mirolla, general editor
Sonia di Placido, editor
David Moratto, interior and cover design
Guernica Editions Inc.
287 Templemead Drive, Hamilton, ON L8W 2W4
2250 Military Road, Tonawanda, N.Y. 14150-6000 U.S.A.
www.guernicaeditions.com

Distributors:
Independent Publishers Group (IPG)
600 North Pulaski Road, Chicago IL 60624
University of Toronto Press Distribution (UTP)
5201 Dufferin Street, Toronto (ON), Canada M3H 5T8
Gazelle Book Services, White Cross Mills
High Town, Lancaster LA1 4XS U.K.

First edition.
Printed in Canada.

Legal Deposit—First Quarter
Library of Congress Catalog Card Number: 2022945216
Library and Archives Canada Cataloguing in Publication
Title: Winners and losers : tales of life, law, love and loss / Darlene Madott.
Names: Madott, Darlene, author.
Series: Essential prose series ; 203.
Description: Series statement: Essential prose series ; 203 | Short stories.
Identifiers: Canadiana (print) 20220413258 | Canadiana (ebook)
20220413266 | ISBN 9781771837675 (softcover)
| ISBN 9781771837682 (EPUB)
Classification: LCC PS8576.A335 W56 2023 | DDC C813/.54—dc23

For Marcus

For giving me the joy of
a grandchild's chatter and
for forgiving me
the chatter I missed.

~

Contents

Winners and Losers

"Good afternoon, sir."

He paid no attention to her, although Francesca Malotti was standing right behind him in the Stratford theatre ticket lineup, although they had just spent the last two weeks together, on opposite sides of a courtroom, litigating a divorce case. When she repeated her greeting and he kept his silence, Francesca felt mortified.

Throughout the first week of the trial, at almost every break, John Jeremey Johnston, Q.C. had given her a collegial prod: "C'mon, we can settle this."

"No, we can't. Your client should shelve her libido and raise the kids in close proximity to their father. Then we can talk."

His client, Cindy Lampe, having fallen in love with a bus driver, Joe Blanchard, on the run from Toronto to Thunder Bay, had made it clear that no compromise was available. John Jeremey

Johnston, Q.C., with his army of junior lawyers
and articling students accompanying him daily
to the trial, reasoned that the parent-child relationship could be sustained by simply subtracting
mid-week access time and adding it onto extended Christmas and summer holidays: same
net time for Dad and the kids—as if separated
parenting were a ledger sheet—abacus counting
with the minutes and days. Out came maps and
travel times, and talk about how quickly a parent, if he cared, could travel the distance between
Toronto and Thunder Bay.

Her argument was equally simple. Time and
attachments are not fungible. Though she pre-
ferred the word direct—not a direct correlation
between time and depth of the bond. (She liked
to think that a certain directness was her great
strength.) She'd told the court that there is no sub-
stitute, on a moment's notice, for the availability
of a father—in this case, Al Lampe. "How," she
asked, "do you pick up a sick kid from school in
Thunder Bay and get the kid home to Nanna's
kitchen in Toronto for chicken soup?"

What often made her advocacy successful in
Court was not that she was more learned than
her "learned friend," but that she believed in
what she advocated—in this case, the import-
ance of a parent's presence in the daily life of a

child, a presence that is all that stands between any child and the darkness.

⁓

"You see this," she told her young son, Marco, opening the freezer door the weekend before the trial to show him the President's Choice frozen dinners. She pointed to the written instructions on the packaging. "As long as you can read, you will never starve." She showed Marco how to turn on the oven, gave him the keys to their home.

The first night of the trial, struggling with her briefcases at 8 o'clock in the evening, Francesca had come home to the smell of shepherd's pie, a candle lit for her on the dining room table, a glass of wine poured, her son practicing the piano.

"Do I have to do this all over again, tomorrow, Momma?"

The second day of trial, her secretary walked across Bond Street to St. Michael's Choir School to pick up Marco from the playground and she put him in a cab for home, this time with Chinese take-out on his lap. Toward the end of the first week, he'd found his own way home by subway and then bus, starting his journey with the older boys from the Choir School, growing independent as he facilitated his mother's work, the two of them making a team together, helping each other survive her absence from his normal life, the ordeal of this trial.

The last night of the trial, she stayed at the office until one o'clock in the morning, writing the closing argument she would hand up to the judge the next day, in bound form and on a memory stick. She'd used her computer throughout the trial, where John Jeremey Johnston, Q.C. had used his juniors and students. There was something almost threatening about the old lawyer. Though he was a very short man, close to only five feet tall, he had presence, bull-shouldered gravitas that bordered on menacing, even dark. Perhaps it was in the thickness of his neck.

But, of course, if there was something really to be feared in him, it was that what he wanted done, wanted to have happen, he had the senior lawyer's ability to make happen, to impose by means of the delegated, sloughed off mountain of work his army of articling students and junior lawyers accomplished, after hours and before dawn, without distraction or conflicted priorities. She, operating alone, on "her own two feet" (she had a habit of planting her feet squarely and solidly, as if ready to withstand assault), had kept calling home, urging her son to go to bed. But Marco had remained up, all the lights on, waiting for his mother, of an age when it was illegal for a parent to leave a child at home alone, untended. The irony was not lost upon her. If Marco told his father about this, there would be a call to the police and then the involvement of the Children's Aid Society. Marco's father fought her at every opportunity. Yet she didn't dare ask Marco not to tell. Sometimes risks had to be taken. She just had to trust Marco. She had to trust to the protective walls her son built around both his houses, the fact that Marco was not a snitch. Marco knew his Momma would come home. He knew that, unfailingly.

Francesca had to feel the visceral grip of the outstretched hand in every case before she could take on the fight. In this case, she'd felt the grip. She honestly believed that parenting took sacrifice. She believed that even a separated mother like herself doesn't get to just move away. A mother must be, if not actually there, then close to that. At the very least, a father must be able to get there, to be on immediate call. She knew the other lawyers, even the judge, felt this human truth. The intensity with which she litigated her cases, she had been told, crossed boundaries, was unprofessional.

"You take the law too seriously. You care too much." It wasn't the law she cared about. It was men and women caught up in the vortex of their personal dramas. She'd never learned not to care.

"Good afternoon, sir."

Nothing.

She would never have expected this of John Jeremey Johnston, Q.C., not for a man of his bearing and public aplomb, and certainly not here, in the Stratford ticket retrieval line-up. On this day, of all days? The day after his defeat at the hands of herself, a junior counsel.

After the trial, Francesca had ridden her bike downtown, to clean up her office and get on top of the other work that had accumulated over two weeks. Marco was with his father for the weekend. Work was the only way she knew how to staunch the pain of her own separation. She spent every alternating weekend working 12-hour days until the weekend was over and Marco returned. Inside her office, on this particular Saturday morning, she could take working no longer. She thought she would suffocate.

❧

She left the bike in her office and walked to Dundas Square.

She ordered a rush ticket to *All's Well That Ends Well*, and then a bus ticket to Stratford.

On the bus she learned there would be no same-day return. She was free, therefore, to stay in Stratford for the weekend.

Her problem became where to stay.

A fellow passenger gave her the phone number for the Stratford Board of Trade. While still on the bus, she found an available bed and breakfast, found bus times that would depart from Stratford for Toronto on Sunday and place her back home seamlessly in time to greet her returning son.

At the start of the afternoon performance, on the outside balcony of the theatre, glass of white wine in hand, under a spectacular sky, the trumpets heralded the audience to come inside for the play. Francesca felt a sudden rush of euphoria. Harming no one, she had just run away. No one knew where she was. She had her cell phone and a credit card. No one would be looking for her. For the first time in a long time, she didn't have a care in the world. She had never felt this free.

It was as if she did not exist.

And then, she did not exist.

There was John Jeremey Johnston, Q.C. He was shaming her. But not because she'd won. No. He was shaming her — she was sure — because of his moment of humiliation, a moment in the courtroom caused by an unwitting answer made by her client, Al Lampe.

To prepare Al for cross-examination, she had asked him what the absolute worst thing Cindy, the mother of his children, might say about him as a husband, father, and a human being.

John Jeremey Johnston, Q.C., large in professional presence, bull-like but small, had been honing in on Al during his cross-examination. Anticipating his next question, Al said: "You're going to ask me about those strip clubs on the Queensway, where I took my clients to entertain them. Cindy never had anything to worry about with me or the strip clubs, sir, because — well, sir — men like you and me, of our size, we're not very attractive to women."

He had spoken so respectfully and wholly without guile. Men of our size.

The judge had flipped her pencil. Even the registrar had laughed, along with everyone else in the courtroom. By six o'clock that evening, the laughter, the humiliation of John Jeremey

Johnston, Q.C. had become the story on Law-yers' Lane. When she got back to the office that evening, her partners—full of competitive spite —applauded her.

Francesca Malotti had won. Her theory of the case had prevailed, but only because of how she had argued it: That the kids of a single father should know their father is close by, in the same city, so that he can exercise his infrequent access to them in close proximity to their mother. It was unheard of at the time: that a *de minimus* ac-cess Dad could keep a mother from moving. Vic-tory lasted the space of one weekend.

"Good afternoon, sir."

What she didn't know, as she had stood there in the Stratford theatre ticket lineup, is that she would be served with a Notice of Appeal, first thing on Monday morning—a Notice of Ap-peal which, at that very moment, John Jeremey Johnston Q.C.'s entourage of junior lawyers was drafting.

Over the ensuing months, there would be five appeals on the issue of mobility before the On-tario Court of Appeal. The results of each, on different facts, would be that the mother gets to move with the kids. She would report each of these to Al, her client, until the day he instructed her to concede defeat and allow the appeal to permit the move. He could no longer afford to fight. He was throwing in the towel. And in so doing, his children would judge that their father, by conceding defeat, had abandoned them.

Years later, Francesca Malotti would bump into one of Al's neighbours, who had been a witness at the trial. The neighbour, according to his own judgment of the situation, would tell her what really happened, what became of Cindy and Joe—the bus-driver boyfriend.

During cross-examination, Francesca had questioned Joe Blanchard about his three failed marriages. From Joe's own mouth, all his marriages had turned sour because of his former wives. No admission that bus-driver Joe had played any part in the failure of his three unions. This marriage, he'd insisted, would be different. Cindy was the one. The one he had waited for, all his life.

"She ran from the house in Thunder Bay to a battered woman's shelter, taking the kids with her, ended up living in a basement apartment.

Joe sued Cindy for his entitlement to half of her house in Thunder Bay. They had bought it together with her settlement. Marrying Cindy was his winning lottery ticket. What a loser. Everybody saw it coming. Everybody, but Cindy."

"Why didn't she come back to Toronto?"

"Who knows? Pride? She was determined to make a go of it in Thunder Bay. Your former client Al wasn't much better, not as a parent anyway. No one will talk to him now, least of all his own children. For God's sake, he took up with Cindy's sister in Toronto. She was known to enjoy the odd snort of cocaine. Cindy's sister was the only one who would have him. One of his daughters never spoke to him again, even refused to see him whenever he showed up in Thunder Bay, which was just about never. That kid will dump both parents out of her life the first chance she gets."

"Who was the last person in my room?" Francesca had cried in the hospital. "Who was the last person in my room?"

Hours after her caesarian section, she ran down the hospital corridor to the nursing station. Marco was supposed to be at her breast. Marco was supposed to be with her in the room, but due to the trauma of the birth, he'd been separated from her. High on medication, she was certain that whoever was the last person in her room had stolen her baby.

"You are our patient, too," the gentle nurse said, leading her back to the room. Only then did Francesca realize she was delusional.

The first time she held Marco in her arms, three days after his birth, she looked into his face, the light in his eyes. He gave her a sudden smile, as if to say, "All will be well, Momma, don't worry."

The nurse explained the smile was gas. The second nurse said, "He is an old soul, a very old soul—a spiritual child." While she basked in this explanation for the smile, Francesca said: "Even old souls need their mother."

"And their fathers, too," the nurse said.

The audience settles. The lights dim. Still brooding about the case, the silence of her opposing senior counsel, she is acutely aware of John Jeremey Johnston, Q.C., sitting there in the same darkness as she, hearing the same words, just as they had listened, only yesterday, to the Judge pronouncing judgment on their case. She sits erect, attentive, but it is more like she is watching the words, not hearing them—except for a phrase or two. She remembers only what the King said, weary of the fight, anticipating the moment when he would not be able to wield a sword and would have to surrender:

'Let me not live,' quoth he,
'After my flame lacks oil, to be the snuff
Of younger spirits ...'

In the darkness of the Stratford audience, she wonders how he has heard these words, John Jeremey Johnston, Q.C., her senior by at least three decades, how he is registering their impact, having just lost to a younger spirit. It is an understanding she will not have for at least three decades, when it will be her own flame that will lack oil, when she will be the one facing her own darkness. But for now, anyway, she gets to just be in the audience, knowing that tomorrow Marco will come home, without fail. Knowing she will be there to receive him, without fail. Knowing that the time will eventually come when the child will grow into his own man, when he will not need her anymore. When she will need a different flame to light the way or relinquish it altogether.

The Ceiling Price

That spring when Winston was apprehended at law school by two RCMP officers, I often wondered what I would say if he asked me to testify at his trial. My *Law of Evidence* textbook taught me that "character witnesses" do not testify to personal opinions about the accused, but to the accused's reputation in the community—"the shadow his daily life casts in the neighbourhood." The one thing I could have said with honesty was that Winston was loved by his friends—I, Francesca, among them.

He was a golden, golden man. The sun seemed to shine on him, to follow him around. Even his hair was the colour of ripe wheat. He had a genial face, predisposed to like people, and blue choirboy eyes, which gazed off elsewhere, giving him a placid sleepy look, a look of ease, almost of complacency—as if knowing himself one of life's favoured sons.

It was as if he always knew everything would work out in the end. He would be acquitted, though 18 others would go to prison with sentences ranging from three to 15 years. His marks, that year, would be the rival of my own — for in addition to being handsome, Winston was smart. He would marry the beautiful Maria del Cavalho, whose rich doctor father gave her a Canadian education at the University of Ottawa where she met Winston. Maria travelled every weekend to Toronto, just to be with him. Her Mexican father would subsidize Winston's legal defense. Winston even articled with the defense lawyer who got him off the hook. It would all work out in the end, exactly the way ... well, almost ...

What strikes me now is that his friends, too, behaved the way Winston expected — as if we all believed in him unconditionally. After two years of law school, maybe that was our training — not to prejudge, nor to express a personal opinion. Factual guilt and innocence are not what the system is about. The strange thing is that none of us ever discussed it among ourselves. We kept our distance from each other at the time, as if afraid of revealing what each of us, privately, really thought. We left our class notes in each other's study stalls or at a common drop-off point for the one who had to mail them that week. Wasn't it lucky he just happened to have a friend in each course? Although Winston was the focus of all his friends' energies that spring, his friends never got together, never spoke of his pending trial.

I read in my Evidence text: "The quest for justice is not necessarily synonymous with the quest for truth. It is better to close the case without all the available evidence being put on the record. We place a ceiling price on truth."

Toward the end of April, a week before exams, Winston's trial was interrupted as the Crown waited for a special witness. Winston was released on bail, his surety being Maria del Cavalho's father. Winston returned briefly to law school to try to arrange to write his exams out West, where the trial was taking place.

He phoned me around dinnertime.

"I've come back to what? I don't feel I belong. I don't even know if they'll let me write my exams. It all seems futile. I don't know what to do."

I knew he wanted me to ask him over for dinner. Perhaps because I sensed he expected this of me, I was reluctant to oblige. For one thing, Maria del Cavalho wasn't with him. I thought it might compromise me, if any of our mutual friends ever happened to find out. I also felt vaguely resentful about the idea of taking care of another woman's man. It was less than a week to my own exams. Even if Winston had nothing to do, I told myself I needed the time to study. I suggested he drop over around eight o'clock, after I normally put my books to bed for the evening. We'd down a bottle of wine together and just talk.

The moment I opened the door, I saw how bad it was with him. There was a tightness across his shoulders and the back of his neck constricting his movements. As he walked past me into the room, his breath smelled sour. He was in complete disarray.

He was also hungry. I watched him devour the snack I had prepared of toast and tuna. Without talking. With total absorption. I asked him if he wanted something more substantial to eat. He admitted to being hungry. I had some chicken in the fridge which I had made for my own dinner. By the time Winston came back from the washroom, I had the table set and was dressing a salad.

We talked and talked. We talked so late into the night that all the distant sounds in the building eventually stopped. We did not discuss the trial. At least, it was not apparent to me at the time that we might have been discussing the trial.

That night, Winston told me a great many things. He told me, for instance, that people had always been extremely generous with him. Friends were always giving him things. There was this trip he had made to England as the result of an invitation from a friend who had paid for everything. All Winston had to do was to bring him this little box. Winston initially thought the free trip was because the friend was lonely, that his friend wanted company — a pal to travel with around Europe. His friend even bought him stereo speakers in England to take back with him to Canada. And now that friend was one of the co-accused in the drug trafficking conspiracy case.

The other thing Winston told me was about a book he had read as a kid on making secret codes. Winston made up such a code, just for the mental exercise, the way people do crossword puzzles. This code he had kept. Kicked it about among his personal belongings for years. He'd never thrown it out; it was based on the word "heroin."

I would have forgotten these things had I not read them later in the transcript of his testimony and recognized them as details he had told me that night. I thought at the time our conversation had centered on men and women: Winston telling me about the women in his life, I about the men in mine. It never occurred to me then, as it has in retrospect, that he might've been rehearsing his testimony.

Winston told me about a woman he had known before he met Maria del Cavalho. They had lived together and then Winston went north to the Yukon to try to make some fast money. During his absence, she left him for another man. She told Winston it was because she thought he would never make it financially. Later, when she learned Winston planned to become a lawyer, she changed her tune. He called her up every now and again and took her out. Finally, she asked him directly: "There's never going to be anything between us, is there?" "No," he answered honestly, "never any more than what there is." They were just one-night stands. He confessed he'd done this almost by way of revenge as he knew it hurt her. He had played with her.

His telling me that disheartened me. I didn't like knowing this about Winston, about men.

I sat with him while he ate and had another glass of wine. By then I was feeling hungry too. I cut some cheese and salami. When that was gone, I put on some tea and brought out the last of my mother's Christmas cake. Winston had three slices. It gave me pleasure to watch him eat. I noticed the rigidness across his shoulders had begun to loosen. He asked if I had a heating pad or hot water bottle that he could borrow that night. I said I would be glad to loan him my heating pad. Was there anything else he needed? He jumped at the offer and asked if he could have a few slices of bread for the next morning.

Then he set his plate away from him on the table and looked at me. He had a decision to make. His lawyer did not think he should testify.

"You want my opinion?" I said flatly. "Take the stand ... unless you've got something to hide."

I could see from the way he bristled that he didn't like my answer.

"That's the way the jury is going to see it," I said. "Whatever the legal theory about your right to remain silent, the human reality is to wonder: 'If he didn't do it, why doesn't he speak?' Besides, think how you'll feel if you don't, then get convicted. You will always wonder if that didn't make the difference, the fact you remained silent."

There was another thing, he told me. None of his co-accused were going to testify. If he alone took the stand, it would put pressure on them all. Some of these people were his friends. It would be a betrayal.

"You'll have plenty of time to regret your loyalty behind bars. Friends, who are they really?

What about Maria del Cavalho? She's stuck with you, through the worst of it. Your first loyalty is to her."

Winston left after three in the morning. As I saw him to the door, he turned and hesitated in the Assiniboine campus hallway. "I will think about what you said. Your advice ... about testifying." I held my hand out for him to shake. He took my hand, but then surprised me by bending over to give me a kiss. It was a chaste kiss — that, almost of a brother — but there was something else about that kiss too.

I had gravitated toward this man in those early weeks we attended classes together, wrote our first case briefs together, went grocery shopping and swimming together. I remember the way he looked at me as I pulled myself from the pool, wet bathing suit clinging to my dripping breasts. He had looked at me the way a man looks at a woman.

That was before I knew Winston had a girlfriend, Maria del Cavalho, that they were engaged to be married. Maria arrived from Ottawa the next weekend. I saw her tired profile as the bus pulled onto campus, the eagerness with which she leapt up to pull her little suitcase from the luggage rack. Then, I saw Winston walking over to meet her.

After that, Winston and I studied together at times, but the terms were different between us.

Standing at the door, I saw a look of fondness in his eyes, saw that he felt a little sorry for me, too. That surprised me because he was the one standing trial — not I, Francesca. Perhaps that night I needed to be kissed. I'd gone to bed even feeling grateful. But later, I tossed and turned. Finally, I wept. Looking back, I must have resented him for what he had so carelessly awakened in me.

In late August of that year everyone returned to campus for the commencement of our final year in law school. I had received one letter from Winston over the summer, so I knew he had been acquitted.

Winston showed up about a week into classes. He called one afternoon to say he was back — that he had some clippings of the trial he wanted to show me. I asked him over for tea.

When I opened the door, he walked right past me into my living area carrying a briefcase and papers stuffed under his arm.

We sat down opposite each other. There was an awkwardness between us. Then, one by one, Winston began handing me the clippings, all of which he expected me to read. The print swam with names of European countries, people and dates, details of some drug conspiracy. What did he want from me? The entire time I stared down at the newsprint, Winston narrated. He spoke of people by name, as if I would know them. He told me about an elderly couple who had been sentenced to 15 years. They were the nicest people, he said. They didn't have any children of their own, but their home was always full of young people. They had a house in Switzerland which they would now lose. The worst of it was that their lawyer had let the time pass for appeal. Winston suspected it was because they hadn't paid his legal bill from the trial. The lawyer should be disbarred. And then there was this girl they sent to Kingston, where her husband would not even be able to visit her. Their marriage was finished for sure—with it would go custody of her child.

He spoke glowingly of all those who had been convicted, disparagingly of the judge and the Crown. He said the day of judgment had been a happy day for him, but a sad day, too, because of all the people he knew who had been convicted. I finally cut him short and asked: "Do you really think, Winston, that out of all those people who were convicted, not one of them was guilty?"

His face turned red. He looked furious. All the geniality was gone, the farm boy smile. I caught a glimpse of a Winston I had never seen.

"I'm not going to answer that," he said, "I refuse to answer that question."

"I'm only asking, because if you do believe that, why would you want to come back to law school? Eighteen people tried and convicted, their lives in ruin, and not one of them factually guilty? How can you participate in a process in which you have absolutely no faith?"

This seemed to mollify him somewhat. I saw the anger retreat.

"Law school has been a kind of penance," he said. "I came here to straighten myself out. In return, law school has given me a kind of legitimacy. Anyway, you do not have to believe in a game to learn to play by its rules."

Toward the end of our meeting, Winston pulled the transcript of his testimony from his briefcase. He had noticed it lying around on the prosecutor's desk at the end of the trial, explained he had picked it up when nobody was looking.

"You stole the transcript?" I said. I couldn't help laughing at the expression on his face—such innocent pride.

"What use would the Crown have for it anyway? Besides, it's as good as mine. Those are my words on its pages."

"You know, Winston," I said finally, "You don't owe anyone any explanation."

He looked surprised. "I know," he said slowly. "I suppose I feel everyone is expecting one."

"You probably think people care more than they do. In a month or two, it won't even be a novelty. You'll wonder if it ever really happened."

"I'm beginning to feel that already. It's hard not to be bitter. Here I am, back at school, as if nothing has happened. I could just as easily have been in prison."

"What are you going to do to put this experience behind you?"

"I don't know," he said. He sat back in his chair, and then grinned his old grin. "I suppose I'll make a scrapbook of the clippings."

That night in bed, I flipped through the transcript he'd left with me. I did not want to read any part of it, would not let myself be drawn down into the words. I was just flipping through its pages when a photograph fell out. The subject of the photograph had been magnified many times and, in the process, lost its sharpness. It showed a road bounded by trees, and a little car parked in the centre of the road, and three people. Two were getting into the car, one on the driver's side, a second in behind. A third was standing, looking up the road. Most certainly Winston. He had his white Hudson's Bay jacket slung over his shoulder, and was standing the way Winston stands, with one knee cocked, that sexy male, at-ease stance, gazing off up the road, the way I had often seen Winston gaze off absently when standing with a group, with those slumberous, choirboy eyes. The photograph was stamped on the back as an exhibit.

I had seen him in that Hudson's Bay jacket a thousand times, with its bold bands of red, green, and yellow. One night I was crossing campus, when Winston and Maria del Cavalho got off a bus together. He had gone downtown to meet her. That night, the snow around them was blue and vast. It was bitterly cold. He wore his Hudson's Bay jacket and carried her suitcase. She had on a thin navy coat, but no scarf. Her neck looked pale and exposed. Hunched inside her coat, she seemed small, as vulnerable as a little sparrow. In his heavy Hudson's Bay jacket, with his fair hair, Winston gave the appearance of a great white snowbird.

The next day I asked Winston about the photograph of him in the transcript.

"That wasn't me in the photograph," he said. The Crown had tried to contend that it was, but his lawyer had set them straight. Did I notice how blurry the photograph was? It had been taken on university endowment lands with one of those telescopic lenses by some investigating officer hidden in the bush. "The lengths these guys went to ..."

And then he said again: "That wasn't me in the photograph."

"Francesca never wears blue jeans," Winston explained to Maria del Cavalho. They had been on a bus, coming back onto campus before any charges, before any trial. "There's Francesca," Maria had said, pointing me out from the bus window. "That can't be Francesca," Winston reportedly replied. "Francesca never wears blue jeans."

I was wearing blue jeans the night I took my mother to a campus movie and bumped into Maria del Cavalho — blue jeans, a white blouse, silver earrings and a thin silver belt. I felt casual and sexy. I have always felt sexy in jeans, although it's true, I seldom wear them. I left my mother with Maria del Cavalho and went off to buy popcorn, when Maria told my mother the story about the blue jeans, who then told me. Hearsay. Maria also told my mother that Winston had so much respect for me. "He thinks Francesca is intelligent.

Whenever we're together, they always talk about the law. They have so much in common."

I did sometimes wear blue jeans. Winston was wrong about that just as the Crown was right about that photo of Winston in a Hudson's Bay jacket.

Winston's friends, the ones whose study notes had gotten him through the year, gave Winston a party in the fall, to celebrate his acquittal. Each of us brought something to the meal and the table overflowed. But it turned out to be a quiet affair. Everyone commented on how tired we all seemed; law school must be making us boring— not even close to exams and already spent, after one glass of wine. I spoke to Winston only once during the evening, sat beside him, on a chair that was a little higher than his. There was a lamp beside his head; when he looked up at me, his face was circled in light. How blessed he is, I thought. All these people gathered around him, all Winston's friends. There was no accounting for our being in the same room together, but for Winston. And in fact, we would never again be together after law school.

Winston was telling me something, his voice

concentrated and serious, but hard to hear above the voices and music of the party. He said he had been thinking about my question, about how he was going to get closure on this experience of the trial. He said he had been turning my words over in his head. I remembered him standing in the silence of my Assiniboine campus hallway, telling me he would think about what I had said, about testifying. It was irresistible. I felt such tenderness for him that I had a sudden impulse to reach out and touch his hair. This impulse was maternal, as if I had something to do with his very presence in the room, his acquittal. He looked at me and smiled. I suddenly realized what it was Winston's friends loved about Winston. I knew for certain there were some in that room who had their own opinions about his guilt. But Winston himself would never suspect us of the thought. He truly believed in our innocence, in what he had said about the gifts of his friends.

The Law Society of British Columbia wouldn't call Winston to the bar. It remains at the discretion of a Law Society to withhold the grant of a license to practise if the Society determines the student's conduct "unbecoming" of the profession, just as it remains within the purview of a Law Society to revoke a license, once granted. The Law Society of British Columbia must not have believed enough in the results of its own criminal process to equate acquittal with innocence, for it found Winston "unfit" to become a lawyer. Worried that Winston might appeal its administrative decision, the Law Society of British Columbia went a step further. It approached his co-accused, then in prison, offering them an early parole in exchange for any damaging information they might provide at the Law Society hearing. Without courtroom rules of evidence, every type of innuendo and smear would have been thrown up, all under the white glare of publicity. Even if, in the end, Winston did succeed in being called to the British Columbia Bar, his victory would have been empty, for what sort of reputation would he have left? But there was a more practical and pressing reason: he would have had to pay not only his own legal fees, but the Law Society's costs incurred as a result of the inquiry. Winston could not afford to continue to fight.

In the letter he wrote to inform me of his decision not to appeal the Law Society's ruling, Winston made a remark that astonished me:

… Life takes many twists and turns. At my core, I have always been hopeful. I believe in destiny and guardian angels. I'm approaching some venture capitalists. My father-in-law has already indicated his preparedness to invest. British Columbia has abundant natural resources, and the best of these is water. I'm developing sparkling water in fruit flavours. When I'm C.E.O. of Mountain Springs Fruit Nutritious, I'll say, "Fuck you, with thanks" to the Law Society of British Columbia. The Benchers might withhold my call, but they can't take away my law degree nor my intelligence. A kick in the behind is a kick-start forward. I'll be on top of my own mountain, drinking my own liquid gold in fruit flavours, looking at those little pin-striped bastards, down below, and what they'll look like will be miniscule. Now that I'm through explaining all the above, I can get on to what's really important — my beautiful newborn son. He really could not have come at a more welcome time.

Unlike Winston, I became a lawyer. But perhaps not the lawyer I set out to be.

Not long after my call to the bar, I represented an old rabbi. The rabbi had got himself entangled in the affairs of a hugely successful family business that he operated with an iron fist and a personal code that was ethically unique. For two days I sat in a closed room listening to the rabbi give sworn testimony when a routine question arose as to document identification and the validity of certain guarantees. The rabbi swore, under oath, that the guarantees were invalid, as not having been signed by the family members whose names they bore. Well, who had signed them? It turned out the rabbi had signed them all himself—some with his left hand, some with his right.

Opposing counsel and I were caught completely off guard.

Red-faced and choking, I called for an immediate recess. Inside the washroom, I laughed helplessly. The rabbi did not have the slightest clue about the import of his words, that what he said or did might have been wrong. Under oath, he had sworn to the truth. He had forged the signatures of his family members. He didn't say "forged," of course. He didn't even understand it as that. In his own ethical universe, he truly believed that by signing their names with his own right and left hands, he had protected them, had invalidated their guarantees. Looking into his blinking, disingenuous eyes, I realized the truly innocent never suspect. It is only the guilty who have this capacity.

Even more unsettling to me was his explanation once I grilled him on the point in my private Law Chambers. He said he had been following my instructions: I had told him to tell the truth.

This silenced me completely. If I had counselled such a thing, how to explain to the rabbi my concern now? As a professional advocate, it isn't only the truth, but about casting the truth in the best possible light. Someone else and not I will be the judge of what that truth might truly be. This is the system, a system in which I profess to believe, which probably works, most of the time, in which I collaborated on becoming a lawyer. So, with that, I comforted myself with the wisdom of Winston: "You don't have to believe in a game to learn to play by its rules."

What I didn't know then, as I do now, is what this does to you over time. What it does to you in that most sacred and private of places—your very own heart of hearts—the all and nothing you take to your grave and where ultimately there is no ceiling price.

Betrayal

Her name was Margaret Meanie.

Those were the days when the big law firms wooed their articling students as the next recruitment of indentured slaves, and the students sought the favours of their senior partner providers. Students articled to law firms are the bottom rung of the legal ladder, only one step above students in law school, but beneath everything else in the climb toward partnership and financial success. The firm hosted monthly dinners at private men's clubs around Toronto. Exceptions had begun to be made for women "guests" of male members. Margaret Meanie and I were two female articling students out of five female students. The articling students numbered 20, in total.

The senior partner in the tax rotation counselled me not to accept a cigar at the end-of-articling Yacht Club dinner, as my female predecessors had before me, not one of whom achieved hire back. The Yacht Club party functioned to welcome in the new coterie of articling students and sail out the old. The labour senior partner counselled me not to stand up after dinner and tell a joke, but to maintain silent composure as a lady should. He quoted from King Lear: "Her voice was ever soft, gentle, and low, — an excellent thing in woman." So I knew, by that early stage, tax and labour (no cigars, no jokes) were already wooing me, wishing me to succeed in the ways of their world.

Margaret Meanie, fellow articling student, with whom I shared a cubby-hole of space adjacent to the corridors of power, took me in hand during our first rotation. She brought me to Harry Rosen's, where I purchased the female equivalent of a tailor-made grey business suit — a skirt, no trousers. She taught me how to tie a feminine bow around my neck and underneath the collar of my pink shirt. The old codger at the table next to ours in the underground bank tower food court smiled indulgently as Margaret reached across the table and undid the bow, aggressively, with a single snap. She had me do up the bow, over and over again, until I got it, just so. And I permitted this tutoring although I was ten years her senior and a mature student. I took my mentorship from the younger women not the men. When I'd attended undergraduate studies, becoming a lawyer was inconceivable. I was reading French literature in the Kelly library over the weekend while the men in our graduating class sat the LSAT entrance exam and counted myself lucky, never appreciating the fact that the men thought the women were attending university only to achieve our MRS. If I'm dating myself, well, I'm hoping this is dated. But somehow, I think not.

"You can't wear slippers," Margaret Meanie counselled. "Not even in our articling office, and certainly not to go to the washroom on the 52nd floor, or any other floor, even if carpeted, with those bedroom poodles on your feet."

Wearing slippers was as much a product of my Italian mother, her clean obsessed plight to save the carpets from dirt tracks when wearing street shoes indoors, as a preference for personal comfort. Instead, I was to wear my Lady Diana flats, at all times, to assume I would be under constant surveillance. Ever vigilant, I was to "dress for the enemy."

It never occurred to me that Margaret Meanie was counselling her own enemy, and why was she doing this? Because all the articling students were in fierce competition with each other. Perhaps it was to lull me into a false sense of security.

The powers-that-be had already seen me with those bedroom poodles on my feet. I was likely already doomed.

The significance of hire-back meant being hired back as a junior associate after the articling year. It meant free court gowns, paid law-society dues, full salary during the bar admission course —seductions the chosen could rarely resist having starved for the four years prior to this achievement. Unless you were the child of privilege, of which I was not.

I was a mature student who left the workforce at twenty-eight to enter law school. I was a sign painter's daughter who lived in a tiny apartment which accommodated a family of five above the sign shop, United Signs and Outdoor Advertising. I worked as an undergraduate summer student on an assembly line at the Kodak Camera Factory. During law school, I bicycled to Ferlisi Brothers to buy chicken backs for soup which sustained me through the week. Hire-back should have been huge. If I valued money as a top priority.

How I had achieved articles in the first place, now occupying this tiny space with Margaret Meanie, in the hallways of privilege, remains a mystery to me, attributable only to my marks and the persuasiveness of the professors who had recommended me. As for the step from articling clerk to junior associate, I had little expectation of this with more conflict than desire.

I had only landed up in law school on a dare made by my mother. Impatient with my floundering over what I was to do with my life, she had suggested I make something of it, like my friend Irene. My friend Irene was a lawyer.

Shortly thereafter, I stood in queue outside the door where the LSAT was to take place before the faculty of medicine at the University of Toronto. There being only three spots available for walk-ins and being the first of the three, I got to "sit" the LSAT. Or rather squirm through it. Without thinking or planning, I'd had three coffees that morning. Not able to trust the other two in line after me to hold my spot while I used the bathroom, I got into the examination room, took my place at a desk, and missed the first set of questions as a monitor escorted me to the ladies' room upon response to my urgent hand waving. And once there, in the stall, I couldn't pee. I had to leave the door open, as if there were any conceivable way that I could cheat. I likely hold a record for the person with the worst LSAT score to ever get into law school. That prison-like experience of pain and shame ought to have served as warning.

Margaret Meanie was not the least bit conflicted. She made no bones about her panting eagerness to oblige. Whatever that took. There was a weekend she flew all the way to Germany to deliver some package, fancying herself a world traveller, having secured a passport in anticipation of articling. In fact, she spent her entire time on the airplane or waiting at the airport or travelling by cab to a law firm that looked a clone of ours in downtown Toronto. How she put up her hand for every assignment, even the ones that had her slaving in the library on long-holiday weekends when the firm turned off the air conditioning to keep down the astronomic overheads. How I hated those weekends with the arrogant, sadistic lawyers assigning research they didn't need for weeks and demanding it be on their desks first thing Tuesday morning. They had licked boots and kissed ass. Why shouldn't we?

Then one day during articles I was called into the corner office of one of the big guns and asked if I knew the history of the wrought-iron gates surrounding Osgoode Hall. Why were they shaped the way they were, so that you entered by wedging yourself right around a vertical turnstile, then left to emerge on the other side of the wrought-iron gate. Even getting through with a litigation briefcase was difficult.

"No," I answered honestly.

"Stupid," Mr. Big-Wig hollered at me. I stood up burning, fully intending to resign my articles and stormed out of his office. Before I could close the door, I heard him bellow after me, "Send in the next idiot." Mr. Dufraine intercepted me, brought me into his own office and calmed me down.

"Ms. Malotti, you don't want the prize for knowing the answer to that question. But you should know, anyway." So, Mr. Dufraine gave me the answer: "It was to keep the cows from entering the gardens of Osgoode Hall when Osgoode Hall was surrounded by farmland as the gates kept the cows from passing around the turnstiles."

"Mr. Big-Wig likely can't either." We both laughed.

Then Mr. Dufraine told me the prize for knowing the answer. It was to take one of Mr. Big-Wig's clients on a walking tour of downtown Toronto, and then off to the jewellery section of Eaton's to help Mr. Big-Wig's client buy his wife a string of pearls. The client always bought pearls whenever he came to Toronto.

Margaret Meanie emerged beaming from Mr. Big-Wig's office. She was thrilled to report, later that day, that Mr. Big-Wig took the client to lunch at the historic Campbell House, across from Osgoode Hall on the west side of University Avenue as she had been asked to lunch with them. During lunch, the client showed off the pearls Margaret had helped him select.

I had given her the answer concerning the turnstiles and the cows.

This kind of indignity wasn't reserved for only the female articling students. Two of the strongest males were asked to off-load a partner's rare-wine collection down at the Toronto docks and given a few bottles for the privilege. Another male student was asked to bring a partner's forgotten jockstrap to his tennis and racket club for his game of squash. The difference was that some of us recognized the indignity, others did not.

The hire-back selection went like this: the articling students noted their preferences for the various legal departments as first, second, third, and so on. It was allegedly a matching program. If tax, labour, real estate, or litigation matched the student, then it went to the back room, and the names of the victors emerged after a night's heated discussions among the articling-student-hire-back committee. The students were never privy to the conversation although painfully aware as to when the selection was taking place in a similar manner that animals must surely be aware once they're gathered to approach the stockyards for slaughter.

Somehow, we knew whether we were going to make it or not.

We knew, for example, that the darling in litigation had already been chosen. The darling had been given three rotations in litigation, to accommodate a trial, and this was clearly an exception to the mandatory single-rotation rule. So we knew litigation was off-the-table if you wanted to be hired back.

We knew that labour was not hiring. Margaret Meanie had her first rotation in labour. We never questioned how Margaret Meanie knew this. I had spent my first rotation in real estate, where I had a nosebleed every time I had to attend the registry office or a commercial real-estate closing; the only good thing about these closings being the free lunch. I thought I would die of nosebleeds, if ever confined to real estate, notwithstanding all the perks of hire-back.

So, although we all somehow knew our inevitable outcome, some of us went to the slaughter and sabotaged it for ourselves as it was less humiliating that way.

I wanted only to litigate. Why I so wanted to

litigate is beyond me. Yes, I had been the only student in my section at law school to win on my side of the moot. Yes, I liked the drama of the courtroom. But I never really thought of myself as competitive in the way that success in a large firm seemed to demand. But maybe I never really knew myself.

There was a game my cousins and I used to play as kids in my grandmother's basement that said a lot about me from a very early age. My grandmother disliked children; even more than children, she hated the noise we made. So my male cousins devised a game we played in my grandmother's basement on Christmas Eve, which was virtually soundless and involved winners and losers. The four youngest cousins, of which I was the very youngest, stood side by each, facing the four oldest cousins, our partners at the game. The four youngest extended our arms. The four oldest took one book from four equally weighted stacks of books in descending order, from lightest book to heaviest, then, placed one book simultaneously upon our little outstretched arms above the wrists. This stacking of books continued, slowly, painfully, and in unison, until one of the four book-bearing cousins collapsed. The cousin to hold out the longest won for herself and her partner. My cousin

Anthony always placed his bets on me and always took me as his partner.

"I knew you'd never give up. It had nothing to do with your age or your strength."

I put litigation as my first and only choice. I knew, with the litigation department having already chosen its darling, I had just slit my own throat. That night my choice coincided with Pierre Elliott Trudeau's walk in the snow. The same night prior to Trudeau's resignation from Office of The Prime Minister of Canada. It was the eve of a final April snowstorm. After the subway ride north, I walked to my junior one-bedroom apartment in my Lady Diana flats — the snow up to my ankles, my shoes ruined, and nylons raddled. I was overcome with a feeling of utter euphoria and liberation. I had just said fuddle duddle to the big firm on Bay Street.

A crestfallen labour partner greeted me on the morrow. Why had I not selected labour? Why had there been only one — out of all 20 articling students?

"We heard, we all understood, that labour wasn't hiring back."

"Where did this rumour start?"

And then his second question when I did not answer the first: "Would you have chosen us, if you had known our department was hiring?"

I hesitated a moment.

No. Labour would never get me into court. I wanted to be a litigator. Much as I respected and appreciated this mentor from the labour department, I was cutting the cord.

Margaret Meanie wrote me some months later after her trip to Ireland: "You must visit that fabled isle. To see the land of W.B. Yeats, the land of Parnell, the uncrowned King, the land of Ireland's heroes, hear the music of the Celtic voice."

I paid for my own trip to Italy that summer with the money I had saved by brown-bagging my lunches. I took that trip to Italy on my own dime, when Margaret Meanie got to go to Ireland that same summer on full salary paid by the firm. Free of the worry of student debt was Margaret Meanie, having been hired back as the labour department's junior associate.

Of course, I would not betray her, strategic wench that she was. She who had taken me in hand and made me buy the grey suit, the pink shirt, the five bows, one bow for every day of the week. If I betrayed anyone over the next thirty-five years, it was only myself.

The Question

When I burned in desire to question them further, they made themselves into air, into which they vanished.
— Lady Macbeth, reading a letter in which Macbeth speaks of the salutations of the weird sisters. ***Macbeth***, *Act 1, Sc. V.*

I was a young woman, then—single and without child—green in the practice of my profession, when I had this dream: a great litigator gave me a powerful secret—the one question that, when asked, would unlock all the secrets of another's soul, heave truth to lip, compel any witness to tell everything. There is a cardinal rule among litigators that's hard to reconcile with the purpose of the question in my dream: never ask a question in cross-examination for which the answer is unknown. Litigators must never let a personal curiosity impair their control of the case. The unknown answer is dangerous and unpredictable. In the art of cross-examination, it is the questions that matter more than the answers.

The Toronto apartment building where Edna Hamilton lived was old and dingy. As we climbed the stairs to Edna Hamilton's apartment, my winded boss, Jack, said how he hated "these airless hallways." His secretary had told me to meet him down at the Y.M.C.A. at 8 o'clock in the morning after his exercise class. He had a file for me that "wanted a woman lawyer." We went to a door, knocked, and an old woman answered. She could have been anyone's grandmother.

There was no air conditioning. Although it was early morning, Edna already had the venetian blinds closed and the burgundy with green floral curtains drawn across the blinds to keep out the summer's heat. Everything was meticulously neat, exactly what one would expect of an old woman's apartment. It was as if Edna Hamilton had moved in thirty years ago when the building was new and everything within her four walls had stayed still in time while the building had run down around her.

Jack reviewed the statement of claim with which Edna Hamilton had been served.

She was being sued by a dead man's estate for the return of some $82,000, plus interest. The claim alleged that the money had belonged to Frank Duvaliers, Edna's now deceased brother-in-law. The executor was one of the many step-sons the dead man had collected through his multiple marriages. The executor wanted the money back for the benefit of Frank Duvaliers' heirs, of which he was one, of course.

"The money wasn't Frank's. Frank never had two nickels to scratch. It was Jeannette Bell's. My dead sister's child. She gave it to me seven years ago — to keep it out of Frank Duvaliers' clutches, no doubt."

"Do you have the cancelled cheque?"

Edna produced a copy of a cheque she had obtained from the Jefferson Bank, Louisiana. It was dated seven years earlier, in the amount of $82,672.35. The cheque clearly stated that it was to the order of our client Edna Hamilton by the remitter, Jeannette Bell.

"There's your defence," the great litigator Jack told me. "Gift from the niece. Never was Frank's money. The Estate has no greater claim to it than Frank would, if alive. You draft the defence."

Then he warned me before he left: "Make sure you get the whole story."

Throughout the balance of that day, I listened to what I thought was Edna's story: "He murdered my sister. Over my dead body will any of that crowd get one cent. Dead or alive, Frank was nothing but trouble ...

"She was 18 when she married him, my sister. We lived on the same street, in Perth, Ontario. Thick as thieves, we were, my sister and I. Jeannette was her first. There was a baby every year after that. I was pregnant, myself, when Frank brought me the news. 'If you ever want to see your sister alive again,' he says, 'come with me now.' I didn't know what he was talking about. I grabbed my coat. I had to run to keep up with him as we climbed the hill to the hospital. Then I saw her. A tube from every hole. Just the day before she'd opened her front door to me with a baby on her hip. She dropped the diaper she held, and we both went down to pick it up together. She smelled of milk and powder, my sister. I remember it like yesterday. A mother with three babes, and yet a babe herself. There was breast milk on some of the blouses I washed after the funeral. That wasn't her in that hospital bed—hair pasted to her face, eyes sunken in like she was already dead. 'Bring me my babies,' she says to me, 'one at a time.' I had time just to kiss her, no time to ask a question. I ran back down the hill to the house again. I called for Jeannette to hurry quickly and put on her coat. Jeannette was just over three.

"Jeannette ran into the room, but when she saw the hand, she drew back from her mother. It had a needle taped to it. 'It's all right,' my sister says to Jeannette, 'Mommy's just going to sleep now,' and for the longest time, it seemed as if she had just gone to sleep. I had to take Jeannette away, finally. Just as we were leaving the room, my sister spoke again. 'Take care of my babies.' Those were the last words she ever spoke to me. She died while I was bringing her boy up the hill.

"'I never knew it would kill her,' was all Frank Duvaliers ever had to say about it. That was years later. Thirty years, when I finally caught up with him. He took off the day after the funeral with my sister's kids. I paid for the funeral. I paid for her plot. I paid for the rent that was overdue on their ramshackle of a house. I washed and ironed and sold or gave away my dead sister's clothes. I paid for the debts Frank Duvaliers left behind. Frank got away with murder, he did. Because that's what it was. She was only 21 at the time."

There was a long bitter silence. Then I asked: "Why did he leave?"

"Why do you think?" Edna blinked at me through indignant eyes, as if to say, how could I be a lawyer and woman, yet not know this?

"Abortion was illegal at the time. The hospital knew what had been done. He put her there. The police were probably just waiting until after she'd been buried."

"How did you find him?"

"Now there's a story. New Orleans. Thirty years on, I had time to kill between bus connections. I was looking through the phone book. I used to look for his name whenever I went to a strange city. Sure enough, there it was. I called the number. Frank was curious enough to invite me over. He had them all gathered at the house by the time I got there. Of course, they weren't babies anymore.

"They all wanted to hear about their mother. Frank had told them she died in childbirth. But Jeannette couldn't remember any baby. Wouldn't she, at least, have seen the baby? She was sharp as nails, that one. She even remembered asking at the graveside, 'What happens when she wakes up? How will she get out?' She remembered the question, but not what anyone answered. Can you imagine asking such a thing? She even remembered the hospital and the trip up the hill. She told me she had cried the first time it rained.

'That made two of us,' I'd said. But by then, they'd have been somewhere in the eastern United States. It must have rained a different day.

"We were doing dishes in Frank's kitchen, me and Jeannette, when I told her the truth. Just then, Frank came in the kitchen. 'I didn't think it would kill her,' he says. And I knew, then, for sure, what I'd only suspected for years."

"What did you do?"

"What do you mean, what did I do?"

"Well, did you confront him?"

"We finished the dishes. Me and Jeannette."

But what about the lives in between, the lives of the babes over which Edna was to have taken such care? Had been charged to do so by her dying sister. A deathbed request!

Jeannette was 15 when her father made her strip in the bathroom and beat her with his belt until she passed out. Frank stopped, thinking he had killed her. The beating caused the injury that caused the plastic-vein replacement operation that ultimately killed Jeannette in later years.

Jeannette's younger brother ran away from home at 14 and worked on a farm, until Frank found him and pulled him back. He left again at the legal age of 16.

"The boy is dead now, too," Edna tells me. "Committed suicide at 60. They found him swinging from the rafters of the barn Jeannette helped him build."

The thing about Jeannette was she made a financial success of her life — buying convenience store operations, trading real estate. "She was sharp as nails, that one."

Then there were Frank's marriages. After Edna's sister, Frank married a diabetic widow with three children of her own, who in the end, wouldn't trust Frank to give her the insulin needle. When Frank's second wife died, Frank married her sister who also happened to be his dead brother's wife, then becoming father to more stepchildren. They all called him "uncle."

"Imagine marrying your brother's wife, your wife's sister? It's like incest. There wasn't a crime Frank Duvaliers didn't commit."

Thirty years of catch-up. Another 20 go by. And in the 20, Edna takes the place of Jeannette's mother. Jeannette visits Edna in Canada, coming north from Jefferson, Louisiana, and Edna goes south to visit Jeannette. Jeannette sends

Mother's Day cards on Mother's Day — becoming more of a daughter to Edna than Edna's own.

Jeannette is 53 years of age, Edna over 70, when Jeannette sends the certified cheque to Canada in the amount of $82,672.35, drawn on the Jefferson Bank. No letter. No explanation. Just the cheque. Edna goes across the hallway and shows it to a neighbour. "Do you think it's real?" Then she telephones Jeannette.

"Do what you want with it," Jeannette tells her. "Invest it, buy a house — it's yours."

A few months later, Jeannette goes into hospital for routine surgery on her leg, to have the plastic vein replaced. She dies of a haemorrhage on the operating table.

And now Frank's heirs are suing for the money. They say it was Frank's — all because of a receipt found in Frank Duvaliers' safe after his death.

"How did Frank come by the receipt?"

"He stole it," Edna tells me, without hesitation. "He stole it from Jeannette. He was always stealing from his rich daughter."

"But why a receipt?"

"How should I know how Frank's mind

worked? The foolish man probably thought to take some action on it during his life."

"Where is the money now?"

Edna sits in her chair, her hands neatly folded in her lap. She gives me a level stare, looking amazingly pink and determined for someone over 80.

"It's gone. As far as Frank Duvaliers and his crowd are concerned, there isn't a cent of it left. I'll fight this until there isn't a cent. He murdered my sister. He should have hanged 50 years ago.

I am thrilled by the story, buoyed up by it all day. I return to the office in a froth of indignation — that anyone could sue Edna Hamilton, after all these years, after all she has been through. My boss, Jack, listens to me speak with that Cheshire smile he wears for a case well matched to its counsel, and then asks the simple question that stops me in my tracks: "You believe her?"

"Of course, I do, don't you?"

"Take some advice: Never believe what your own client tells you. That way, you may be pleasantly surprised, but you'll never be disappointed."

The case is mine! I write an outraged letter to opposing counsel and tell him that if the estate of Frank Duvaliers goes away, now, we'll let them off lightly. Should he pursue this spurious litigation, we'll be looking for costs. Opposing counsel writes back demanding dates for the questioning. He encloses documents. Among the estate's documents are two inexplicable letters:

Dear Jeannette,

I've just gotten home from the Toronto Dominion Bank. I have good news for you, Jeannette. The interest rate went up 2% today so you are now getting 15.2% interest on your money. I just can't understand Frank. If he'd left it in the Jefferson Bank, the money would only have lain there at around 9% at most. I think you are much better off with it here. You could have had it in your name had you sent the money directly from the Jefferson Bank to my Bank here, but you would have had to pay American income tax and, also the Bank would have had to deduct 15% of the interest in instalments for Canadian withholding tax because you live outside Canada and are drawing interest from Canadian sources. I will explain it better when I come down.

If your Dad wants to come to Toronto and drop in for a visit tell him, by all means, to come. I am alone and he has no need to worry about any Mr. Hamilton. I still classify as 'single' and I don't care who he lives with or if he goes through some form of marriage. For all I care, he can have a harem if he's man enough.

Aunt Edna

Dear Jeannette,

Just a hasty note asking you to send me back the original receipt I sent you. I must have it to return to the bank when the term deposit comes due. It is wise that you have no papers about where Frank's money has gone. Also, destroy any bank numbers and the bank passbook. It is only good to me, seeing it has my name only on any transactions. If these people are bent on trouble, there's no use giving them any opportunity to find out where Frank's money went. It is Frank's money.

I will not give any part to anyone, only Frank, at the end of five years. He trusted this amount to me, and I will honour that trust to the end.

I did not see my granddaughter. It was a strange thing for her to phone me, seeing I did not know her and really have no desire to be involved with any of these people. I have gotten along all these years without them. Now out of the blue they appear on the horizon. My desire for all my grandchildren is for them to retire back into the sunset and continue to forget me, as have their parents.

Tell Frank to drop in when he comes to Canada.

Aunt Edna

The day before the scheduled examinations, I go again to Edna's apartment to prepare her for discovery. The discovery is a pre-trial questioning, where the lawyers and their clients get to learn the strengths and weaknesses of theirs and the other side's case. Many motions can be brought arising out of discovery, short of a trial, to expedite or abort the inexorable litigation track toward trial. Some motions are strategic or procedural, like motions to compel refused answers, or motions to strike pleadings for failure to answer undertakings, or motions for summary judgment based on no triable issue. These motions can multiply like the proverbial sands of Arabia, and often cases end because litigants run out of money, or because someone has the deepest pocket, or the best lawyer. Like Edna had me.

Preparing Edna, I show her the letters. Edna sits in her chair and reads them silently. After she has finished reading them, she looks at me calmly. Her eyes above the line that separates her bifocals are small and sharp, below the line, swollen and unfocused, like two blobs of runny jelly.

"These letters," I tell her, "are a problem."

"You think they are a problem?"

"Clearly," I tell her. "For example, what did you mean by Frank's money? Why are you accounting to Frank and Jeannette for the interest rate? Why did you send Jeannette a receipt? What's all this concern about tax implications of the transfer if the money was a gift?" I rattle off a whole series of questions relevant to the lawsuit, and then I tell Edna these are the kinds of questions she will be asked on the morrow. But in my mind, there is another question that I have no excuse for asking. Why did you invite Frank to come to you? Your sister's murderer ...

... I am alone ... I am still single ...

"Do you know what I think?" Edna tells me that day, "I think Frank stole the money from his second wife. He was involved in litigation for years, you know, with her kids. They finally got a court order to kick him out of her house. But when they went looking for her money, it was gone."

Only afterwards do I realize I left that day without any answers. But my questions accomplished what they were meant to accomplish professionally: They prepared Edna Hamilton for her discovery.

The Discoveries

Discovery of Edna Hamilton

Q: Mrs. Hamilton, I am showing you a letter dated May 12, 1981. It is addressed to "Dear Jeannette and Frank." Can you identify this, please, as your letter?

A: I have no recollection of writing this letter.

Q: Could you take a moment to look at the handwriting and tell me whether or not you recognize it as your own handwriting?

A: I have no recollection of writing this at all, I am sorry.

Q: I am not asking you whether you recollect writing it. My question to you is, do you recognize the handwriting?

A: The handwriting can't be mine if I can't recollect writing it.

Q: Do you deny that this is your handwriting?

A: I have no recollection of writing this.

Q: I can write a letter and not remember writing it but that does not mean it is not my writing. I am asking you if that is your handwriting?

A: I don't think so.

Q: Are you not sure?

A: I have no idea of ever writing it so therefore I couldn't have written it.

Q: Mrs. Hamilton, I am going to show you another document. Is that in your handwriting?

A: I can't honestly say.

Q: You neither deny nor confirm it?

[Me]: You have her answer, she cannot honestly say. She cannot identify it one way or the other as her handwriting.

Q: Okay. Well, then, I will have to live with that, for now.

But I cannot live with it. I could not live with it then. I cannot live with it now.

Q: Mrs. Hamilton, do you recall telling Jeannette that if her father wanted to drop in and visit, that by all means he was welcome to do that?

A: No.

Q: Did Frank Duvaliers visit you in 1981?

A: No, he did not.

Q: Did Frank Duvaliers ever visit you for the purpose of collecting money?

A: No.

Q: He never did?

A: Never.

[Me]: Did he ever visit you?

A: No, never.

Q: Were you provided with some sort of paper from the bank at the time you bought the term deposit to show that you had a term deposit with the bank?

A: You mean a receipt?

Q: Yes. Were you given a receipt?

A: Yes.

Q: And do you have that here with you today?

A: No.

Q: What became of that?

A: I sent it to Jeannette.

Q: Yes?

A: And that was the last I saw of it.

Q: Why would you send a receipt to Jeannette?

A: Just to show her what I had done with the money, that's all. No purpose other than that.

Q: Did you, sometime before the term deposit matured, attempt to recover from Jeannette the receipt you had sent her?

A: I asked her for it, yes, on the phone.

Q: Did you also send her a letter asking for it?

A: I don't remember sending her a letter. I phoned her all the time.

Q: Why did you want the return of the receipt?

A: Well, a receipt's a receipt, isn't it? No particular reason.

Q: When the term deposit matured, did you not need that receipt?

A: No, I went to the bank, and they gave me another one, but I can't tell you where that is either.

Q: Why would you find it necessary to send Jeannette the receipt when you had already told her on the phone what you had done with the money?

A: Well, just to, I mean, she was like a daughter to me, we didn't keep any secrets or anything from each other, she was like my daughter. Her mother was my sister.

[Me]: Counsel, you might want to ask what reason Jeannette gave for not sending the receipt back to Edna Hamilton.

[Discussion Off Record]

[Back On Record]

Q: Do you recall, Mrs. Hamilton, being visited or attempted to be visited by a granddaughter?

A: No. Granddaughter of whom? My own?

Q: Yes. Do you have grandchildren?

A: I have grandchildren. I don't see them.

Q: How many grandchildren do you have?

A: I would imagine 11 or 12.

Q: And you don't see any of them?

A: No. In fact, I haven't seen them, not even when they were born. I have never seen them. You may find it odd but it's true.

Q: Yes, it is strange.

A: It is strange, but ...

Q: Would you like to see them?

A: No. I have no desire, not now. They're grown up and married.

[Me]: How is this relevant?

Q: You are aware that Frank Duvaliers remarried again subsequent to May of 1981, a person by the name of Margaret Duvaliers.

A: Yes.

Q: And Margaret Duvaliers, she had been married previously to Frank's brother, is that true?

A: That's right. I don't know her, mind you.

Q: And Frank had been married previously to her sister?

A: Yes.

Q: Do you deny that she, subsequent to being married to Frank, in about 1981 or 1982, visited you here in Toronto?

A: Visited me?

Q: Yes.

A: I've never seen the lady. I don't know her, never set eyes on her, never in my life.

[Me]: Let the record reflect my client's surprise.

A: I have never seen her. She was the third wife, you know. The second wife was her sister. And the third wife was married to Frank's brother, before Frank. They're all dead now. Everybody's dead. Except me. [*Laughter*]. Aren't I awful?

Q: Is there any reason you know for why Jeannette would give this money to you by way of gift?

A: I told you, she was like a daughter to me.

Q: And for what period of time had you carried on a relationship with Jeannette that she was like a daughter?

A: About 20 years.

Q: Had she ever given you money before?

A: No.

Q: And did she ever subsequently?

A: No.

Q: Had she ever given you anything else, anything other than money?

A: No, just you know, cards. Christmas cards, birthday cards, things such as that. She never missed an occasion for cards. I have two or three albums here full of them if you want to see.

Q: I would, yes actually if your counsel doesn't mind.

[Me]: Go ahead.

Q: Did you have any conversation with Frank Duvaliers after receiving these funds?

A: No.

Q: Any conversation at all?

A: No.

Q: Either by phone, any correspondence or contact?

A: No.

Q: None?

A: None.

Q: Mrs. Hamilton, you have indicated in your Statement of Defence that there is a family history here that might have bearing on the issues, arising out of the fact that Frank was married to your sister. Your sister died?

A: Yes.

Q: Of what did your sister die?

A: An illegal abortion.

Q: An illegal abortion?

A: Yes.

Q: Did she not undergo an abortion in the hospital?

A: No. Wasn't allowed then, young man.

Q: Do you have any knowledge of where it was that she underwent an abortion?

A: At home.

Q: And where was that at the time?

A: Northern Ontario.

Q: And how do you know that?

A: I lived there.

Q: You lived with them?

A: No. I lived with my husband up the street.

Q: And were you present during the abortion?

A: No. I saw her in the hospital, afterward.

Q: And do you know who performed the illegal abortion?

A: Yes.

Q: Who?

A: Frank Duvaliers.

Q: How do you know that?

A: He told me himself.

Q: He told you himself?

A: Yes.

Q: Now, you wrote in your pleading that your sister had asked you to take care of her children?

A: Yes.

Q: Do you have any indication that Frank was not prepared to take care of his own children at the time?

A: I don't know. My sister asked me to look after her babies. He took them off to Mexico, then to the States, back to Mexico, back to the States.

Q: Did you ever report Frank Duvaliers to any authorities?

A: No, because at the time I didn't know that he was the one who did the abortion.

Q: Now, in your Defence, you say, "It was generally known by the family that Jeannette had given this money to Edna Hamilton." What family are you referring to?

A: Jeannette's.

Q: You are referring to her two children?

A: I think they all knew. I would imagine they would know.

Q: What evidence do you have that it was generally known?

A: Well, I would imagine they did a lot of talking. I don't know. I wasn't there.

Q: Did you touch any part of the principal monies before the maturity date on the term deposit?

A: No.

Q: What did you do with the interest earned on the term deposit?

A: Spent it.

Q: You spent all of it?

A: Yes.

Q: Pardon me?

A: Yes.

Q: What did you do with the principal after the term deposit matured?

A: Spent it.

Q: You spent it?

A: Yes. It was given to me. It was given to me, you know. I didn't steal that money. Understand that, young man.

Q: How did you spend it?

A: Good heavens, I couldn't tell you every place I spent it.

Q: Have you made any gifts to anybody since the beginning of this legal proceeding?

A: I really don't think that is any of your concern. I can do what I like with my money, you know.

Q: Is any of the principal or interest left on the money you say was given to you by Jeannette?

A: Not one cent.

[Re-examination]

[Me]: Edna Hamilton, opposing counsel asked you about a receipt. What was the reason Jeannette gave to you for not having the receipt available to send back to you?

A: Her father had it. Frank Duvaliers stole it out of her papers.

A: Thank you. No further questions.

[Counsel]: Let the record show that during the period of time we were off the record, counsel had the opportunity to refresh her witness on that very evidence.

[Me]: No, let the record reflect that while off the record I indicated to counsel there might

be a question he would want to ask, and
when he asked the question and got the
same response I have just obtained from my
client, he said he did not want it on the
record, and I told him I would ask that
question in re-examination.

[**Counsel**]: We can argue this until the cows
come home.

[**Me**]: In any event, I will have my opportunity
to examine Mrs. Hamilton in chief and we
will get the whole story at the trial.

Frank's funeral must have been an animated
event … It had taken place in Moncton, New
Brunswick. After the burial, everyone returned
to the house which had belonged to his third
wife prior to her death. Those present included
the sole surviving daughter of his first marriage,
Jeannette, and the children of Frank's second
and third wives. Walter, son of the third wife and
executor of Frank's estate, was also there. Imagine everyone's excitement when he went down
into the basement and opened the safe. There
was a shoe box inside. In the shoe box, he found

the letters. Upstairs, gathered around the table, Walter read the letters aloud to all the family members present. He took them to a lawyer the very next day. Everyone wanted to see what should be done about the matter. They all figured it was Frank's money; it should be put back. They all wanted their fair share, this greedy little bunch. I can hardly wait to examine Frank's executor, representative of his estate.

Discovery of Estate Trustee

Q: You'll agree with me, sir, that the last will and testament of Frank Duvaliers appears to have been made some three years after the gift of money to Edna Hamilton.

A: Yes.

Q: Now, I note from the will that Frank was quite specific about bequeathing certain things. For instance, his tools.

A: Yes.

Q: And he also bequeathed a gold watch and ring to a great grandson.

A: Yes.

Q: And a truck to someone else.

A: Yes.

Q: Now, from the statement of receipts and disbursements, you'll agree with me that the total funds in the estate appear to be about $114,000.

A: Yes.

Q: And you'll agree with me that nowhere in the will is there mentioned a sum of approximately $80,000 United States dollars which Frank believed he had as part of his property.

A: No, it wasn't mentioned in the will.

Q: Don't you think that was odd?

A: Well, a little bit, yes.

Q: Why does that strike you as odd, sir, now upon reflection? Is it because it's a large sum of money?

A: Yes, right.

Q: Relative to what was in his estate at the time of his death?

A: Yes.

Q: In fact, it's larger than the sum of money that was available at the time of his death? You'll agree with me?

A: Larger?

Q: Yes, $80,000 U.S. funds at the time he allegedly sent it to Edna Hamilton would be worth a lot more seven years later at the time of his death, converted to Canadian funds.

A: Yes.

Q: And yet no mention of it at all in the will?

A: No.

Q: Now, I'm told that at the time Frank married your mother, your mother had cancer and was, in fact, dying.

A: Not to my knowledge.

Q: But she died, in fact, within a year of the marriage.

A: Yes, that's correct.

Q: What did you think of him?

A: Who, of Frank? You mean personally? I found him a real nice man.

Q: So, you approved of his marriage to your mother?

A: Yes.

Q: Did you trust him?

A: Yes.

Q: Did you generally find him a trustworthy person?

A: Yes.

Q: Did you think he was a rich man?

A: No.

Q: Did you think he was a man of means?

A: I never really thought about it.

Q: Did you assume he had enough money to support your mother?

A: Well, my mother could have supported herself.

Q: At your mother's funeral, did you ever say to Frank Duvaliers: "Where's my mother's money?" Or words to that effect?

A: No. I never said that. I didn't care.

Q: Did your mother have an estate?

A: Yes.

Q: What did that consist of?

A: Her home and her car.

Q: What about bank deposits?

A: As far as I know, she and Frank had joint bank accounts. All the money went to Frank.

Q: You never said to him: "What became of Mom's money?"

A: No.

Q: Is it true that your family — you and your brothers and sisters — made Frank sign his pension over to your mother at the time of their marriage?

A: No.

Q: So, you deny that.

A: Yes.

Q: In fact, the children of Frank's third wife did quite well by Frank's Will.

A: Not really, because a lot of that money was my mother's.

Q: When you say a lot of that money was your mother's, what percentage would you have in mind?

A: I'm not really sure, but when Frank came to Canada, he didn't have that much.

Q: How much did he bring?

A: About $11,000.

Q: So, if we've got about $100,000 in bank deposits at the time of Frank's death, and Frank came to Canada with $11,000, only about 10% of that $100,000 would have been his. The rest was your mother's? Is that a fair statement?

A: Yes.

Q: So, this is a man who comes to Moncton, New Brunswick with about $11,000 to his name. And a few years later he's making a will. And according to your theory of the case, he believes that there's a woman holding $80,000 U.S. of monies that belong to him. And he doesn't say a thing about it in his will. Would you agree with me that's a pretty significant omission?

[Counsel]: I object to that. It's not omitted from the will. Specific reference is not made, but it's not omitted and that is a question of law, which my client is not going to answer.

Q: Do you have any explanation, sir, for Frank's delay — no, it's more than delay — for his failure to ever institute legal proceedings to get this money back during his lifetime, during his remaining seven years?

A: No, I don't.

Q: No explanation whatsoever.

A: No.

Q: Let me put this proposition to you: If those monies were dirty monies, if those monies were stolen, or if those monies would have attracted a criminal charge if the late Frank Duvaliers instituted proceedings to get them back, is there any reason why the estate should be able to prosecute this action with impunity?

[Counsel]: That calls for speculation on the part of my client, and I refuse to let him answer that question.

Q: I would like to know why Frank Duvaliers did not start proceedings to get this money back during his lifetime?

A: The man to answer that question is not here on the earth today.

Q: The man to answer that question is not here on earth, but he apparently has quite a number of spokespersons, judging by the number of people talking after his funeral.

[Counsel]: We'll undertake to provide you with any information we can obtain as to whether the monies were dirty monies. This is the first we've heard of it.

[Me]: Well, no, the first you heard of it was from your own client's mouth, that he was told by Jeannette's sister that Frank was worried about criminal charges.

A: No, I didn't say that. Edna told him that. Jeannette's sister told me that when Frank came with his third wife to get the money from Edna, Edna threatened him that she would lay charges against him for smuggling his money or taking it out of the States or some-such-thing.

Q: The fact remains, sir, that for seven years, to the best of your knowledge, no steps whatsoever of a legal nature were taken by Frank to obtain the return of those monies.

A: Not that I know of.

Q: And you think you can come to court behind the smoke screen of an estate, where Frank couldn't come in his lifetime?

[Counsel]: Don't answer that.

Q: I have information that there was a bank passbook of Frank's second wife among the papers in Frank's shoe box, and that passbook unlocked the mystery that had been tormenting her kids for years, which was probative of the sum of $80,000 having been, in effect, stolen from his second wife's bank account prior to her death. This bank passbook of the second wife shows the withdrawal of some $80,000 — $82,672.35 to be specific, just prior to her death in hospital. Did such a passbook, to your knowledge, show up in the shoe box?

A: Not to my knowledge.

Q: Now, there is a statement which is attributed to Frank's only surviving daughter of his first marriage, regarding the tone after the funeral of Frank Duvaliers — and I quote this roughly: "You should have seen them all arguing like cats and dogs." Would you describe the tone following Frank's funeral as analogous to the arguments of cats and dogs?

A: That's all news to me. I couldn't have been there. I must have been asleep.

Q: How would you describe the tone after the funeral?

A: No different than after any funeral — everybody just sitting around the table talking and drinking tea.

Q: So, there was no dismay about the will? There were no hard feelings?

A: Well, I wouldn't say no hard feelings. Somebody's always bound to be disappointed.

Q: You indicated that your wife received the will from Frank at the time she took him to hospital.

A: Yes.

Q: When he gave it to her, did he tell her that, in addition to this will, there's also the money Edna Hamilton is holding for me?

A: I don't think he did, because I never heard her mention anything like that.

Q: Did he ever, in the time he was in hospital — how long was he in hospital?

A: Three or four days.

Q: Did he, at any time he was in hospital, mention Edna Hamilton?

A: Not to my knowledge.

Q: You indicated that there were some photographs that you came across when you went through the papers. Is that right?

A: Yes.

Q: Were any of those photographs of Edna Hamilton?

A: No.

Q: Or Frank Duvaliers?

A: No.

Q: If you come across any photographs of Edna Hamilton, will you produce them for me?

A: Yes.

[Counsel]: How is this relevant?

As if a picture could tell: Who was Edna Hamilton? Who was Frank Duvaliers? What power did he have over women? Such power that his first wife had not accused him of her death. Was she like the victim in the newspaper I read about, a woman in such deluded love with her murderer that, when her own dying daughter asked her: "Why did you let him do it, Momma, why did you let him douse us in kerosene and light a match?" she answered: "I don't think he knew it was kerosene." Such power that a dying woman would sign a cheque to Frank Duvaliers in preference to her own flesh and blood? Such power that the dead woman's sister took him in when her sister's children got a court order kicking him out of her dead sister's house? Such a power that the daughter he had stripped and beaten in a bathroom at the age of 15 helped him get the money out of Jefferson, away from people "bent on making trouble?" Such power that Edna invited him, her sister's murderer, to herself. "... tell him by all means to come. I am alone and he has no need to worry about any Mr. Hamilton. I still classify as 'single' ..."

Why did Edna Hamilton not report Frank Duvaliers to the authorities? Why had she searched for him for 30 years? Why had she written those words in her letter—"I am alone ... I am single ..."—words meant for a man she believed had murdered her sister? Was it love? Was it hate? Was it revenge? Was it anything one question could illuminate?

Here's what I think must have happened: Edna Hamilton did not take Frank's money. It wasn't Frank's money. It wasn't Jeannette's. It was the money of the dead second wife. Edna was right about that. Because she knew Frank. She knew how Frank lived off women. He'd got his sickly diabetic wife, the wife who didn't trust him to give her the insulin needle in the end, to sign a cheque to him while in hospital. He had to get the money out of Jefferson, using the only people he could trust. He sent it to Edna, using Jeannette. He sent it to Edna. Edna was someone he could trust. How did he know that? Why did he think he could trust Edna Hamilton? Why did Edna take the money? Why did she write Jeannette, "tell him by all means to come"?

The afternoon after her sister's death, Edna went to meet Frank. No one ever knew. She went to him to ask him a question, but all the way there, all the way to that ramshackle of a rented house her dead sister had scrubbed and curtained and filled with the smells of babies and milk, all she could think of was the two of them together —Frank and her sister, how they had looked at each other their first summer in love, what their love had done to her, how it had tormented her in bed at night through a whole summer of rest-lessness, uncovered on the creased sheets, tossing for loneliness until the sound of geese going south released her, a season dead, the earth cool-ing and only beginning to hunger. She married Mr. Hamilton the next spring.

Edna is sitting on the couch; Frank is at the window ... It is the first day after her sister's death. Frank pauses with his hand holding back the curtain, watching something in the street.

His lengthy body with its thick thighs and heavy sex, weight poised on one hip, arms crossed on his sloping chest with the sleeves rolled: his presence, so physical, with its unaroused sensuality. They are both young. Frank pours them a drink. Edna is three months pregnant and knows she shouldn't take it. But she does. As he hands the glass to her, their hands touch.

He stands with one hand in the pocket of his pleated pants. He tugs on the cord of the venetian blinds, sending them crashing. For no reason at all, Edna gives Frank a memory: "When I was a little girl, I used to imagine this dark man who'd come to the house while my father was at work. I'd feel him in the house like a shadow—someone who had always just gone, who had waited for me, who I always missed by staying out a minute longer."

"Was there?"

"Was there what?"

"A man."

"No ... I don't think so."

Frank stares now at the floor as if he can see through it or is listening intently to something in the next room. Edna listens too. They hear only the kitchen clock. A neighbour is taking care of the kids.

"I don't know what I'm talking about." Edna sounds drunk.

"There's a lot you don't know."

"Look, I didn't come here to —"

"Why did you come?"

"Because my sister is dead."

Frank laughs. She listens to his laugh, the sharp cynicism of it driving furrows through the silence, turning her words over like clods of freshly exposed earth.

"You came because you're guilty."

"Why should I feel guilty? What did I have to do with this?"

"You tell me."

Edna rises, looks around the room for her coat. The suddenness of her rising throws her off balance.

Frank puts his hands on her shoulders and pushes her back into her seat.

"Sit down, for Christ's sake. Besides, you don't want to go yet, and I don't want to be alone."

Edna accepts his hands on her shoulders, feels herself grow pink.

"What did you do to my sister, Frank?"

All of a sudden, the risk she has taken in coming occurs to her, makes her want to vomit. Trapped, by this dark front room with its empty traces of her sister still lying about, by the possibility of Frank's violence, by his maleness.

As if he knows why she's frightened, Frank automatically softens. He puts down his glass, and when he looks at her again, the expression in his eyes is completely different, gentler, reassuring, as if he wants her to stay, as if the moment before hasn't happened. She can't believe it.

"Why don't you stay?"

"I can't——"

But she doesn't go. She rises again and stands in the middle of the room, staring at the slates of light in the covered window, waiting, her mind unsettled, as if to go now would leave everything unfinished, as if somehow this isn't enough.

"I feel, I don't know ..."

"I know, I feel the same."

For a moment they stand together, not talking.

"Oh God," he says.

Edna believes she can feel him trembling. The weight of his pain draws her to him.

And then the most unexpected thing begins to happen. Standing together in that room, the absurdity of their standing together, after what has happened, suddenly breaks in on them. Frank and Edna begin to laugh. Caught by each other, laughing almost to tears, avoiding eyes at first and then, the one bitter glance through each other that sobers them both.

The next instant exists in outline, like the cartoon of an inspiration which waits only its execution. For a moment they face each other in silence. The alternative is boredom. The alternative is the years with Mr. Hamilton and five small children, and the long years that follow Hamilton's desertion, of working at three jobs around the clock just to feed and clothe them — those ungrateful kids who will grow up anyway, who will grow up on their own and leave her, too, not knowing who Edna Hamilton was until it almost doesn't matter that she was ever their mother. The alternative is boredom. But Frank and Edna are not bored. They both know it.

She had known then. And wasn't horrified. Intrigued, rather, that such a thing could happen, might even still happen; so fascinated, that standing at the door they are lost in possibility.

He might close the door again … He might take her coat and sling it over the chair. And take her, not scooped under as you'd hold out an offering, but one arm wrapped over her legs, closing her in so that her whole body is turned and hidden from itself against him, moulded around each rhythmic movement of his body toward the bedroom; the first cold contact of sheets, his unfamiliar nakedness, undressed clumsily against her, mouth finding her breasts, her stomach, not leaving her a moment; Edna closing her eyes as he undresses her, and then seized by a sudden panic, struggling underneath him, wanting to hurt, to bite hard, unable to go with his fierce increase of pleasure, finding herself parted — Frank groaning, lowering the whole force of his weight into her, thrusting up into her abdomen. She rises and wraps her legs around his back, her mouth open over his shoulder, his arms curled under her back, hands tugging down on her shoulders; she curves like a cup under his frightening strokes coming down into her until they both reach what she has come for.

Running, running back up the hill, three months pregnant with Hamilton's child, running back to her own safe life. For this is Frank's power — not the body's seduction, not just that Edna had touched him over and over again without really touching, not just sex, the need for which would die eventually, which would have made such a moment, had it really happened, seem ridiculous in retrospect to one as intelligent as Edna, such a waste of time, but that he, Frank, knew her. How had he known he could trust her? He — not bound to Edna's fantasies, the dreams she summoned for herself, the tricks she pulled to get herself privately through the years — Frank showed her, in his eyes, what she was up to all along. He was prepared to be whatever she wanted. He is the knower, Frank Duvaliers, one of her kind—the mask disintegrating in one instant of mutual recognition. Who is this Frank Duvaliers? Who but herself, the mirror of her own possibility.

Until he brought another sister to Canada. Until he chose another sister as his third and last bride. Until she lost the power to self-deceive.

She had never forgiven him that. He ought to have hanged 50 years ago.

"The money's safe with me. I will not give any part of it to no one. Only to Frank at the end of five years." Edna took the money because she knew that Frank would follow it to Canada, that eventually he would come. And he did come. He came to her on route to Moncton. Only he came with a bride, the sister of his dead second wife. It was that—not the murder of her own sister, not the beating of the sister's child, not anything but that—his choice of a different sister when this time she was free, that dissipated his power over her ... I am alone. ... I am single.

That must have been some moment when he asked for his money. When she told him he wasn't going to get any of it, not one red cent.

And if he tried to make trouble for her, she'd make trouble for him. She'd report him to the authorities, for trying to defraud the Canada Revenue Agency and the U.S. Internal Revenue. So, Edna Hamilton had settled for Frank's money. She had let Frank trust her and, in one way anyway, the trust had paid off.

Did any of it happen? Did it happen that way?

I thought I would get the whole story at trial. But there never was a trial. The out-of-province estate failed to post security for Edna Hamilton's costs, and I brought a motion to court to have the claim struck out against her. A strictly procedural conclusion. A perfect result, from a professional perspective. The ones who would ask questions of Edna Hamilton vanished into air.

But had they been permitted to ask, would truth have been the result? In cross-examination, it is the questions that matter, more than the answers. To control the witness, to advance one's own theory of the case, that is the purpose of cross-examination which cannot be reconciled with the purpose of the question of my dream. Is there a single question which could have unlocked Edna's truth?

The last I ever heard from Edna Hamilton was her response to a letter I sent to her niece, when I had gone looking for Edna Hamilton and learn-ed she had moved:

Ms. Malotti:

I am at a loss to hear from my niece that you were looking for me. [As if my very curiosity were impertinent.] I moved to Regina, having heard that my apartment was going to be taken down and there being no reason to stay in Toronto anyway.

I would very much appreciate it if the balance of funds in trust were sent to me direct, since I have no need to go to Toronto at the present time. Thanking you for your able representation of me and trusting to hear from you soon about the money.

Yours truly,
Edna Hamilton

At 85 years of age, alone and single, Edna had packed up and left.

The hand that wrote to me was round and firm. The proportions and shape of the letters appeared to my eye what the handwriting expert had said of Exhibits "A" and "B" when examined against the sample handwriting given at Edna's discovery: "Significantly similar ... consistent with the conclusion that the sample was written by the same person years earlier."

Who was that person? Who do my questions reveal but her questioner—possibilities of self only I have been able to conceive?

Replevin

An action whereby the owner or person entitled to repossession of goods or chattels may recover those goods or chattels from one who has wrongfully distrained or taken or who wrongfully detains such goods or chattels.
 —(Legal Dictionary)

"I wondered when you were going to figure that out," the judge said.

The judge had seen the young lawyer sweating out the list at the back of his courtroom, waiting for an opportunity to re-approach the bench.

Francesca Malotti, the neophyte lawyer, had obtained a Replevin Order, without notice to the art gallery and its lawyer who had wrongfully kept her client's paintings after the artist's demand for their return. The art gallery had sold some without remitting commissions in accordance with the gallery's representation contract. When Francesca's client Chinkok Tan showed up in person at the Harvey Flicker Art Space, demanding to take back his remaining paintings, the gallery owner, Harvey Flicker, had refused and threatened to call the police. Even more worrisome, the doors to the Harvey Flicker Art Space remained closed, the following Saturday. Francesca had to act fast, before the art gallery went bankrupt and Chinkok Tan's paintings became the property of the bankruptcy trustee.

"My client is an artist, your Honour. To require him to post a bond equal to the value of his paintings would be tantamount to requiring him to buy back his own creative work! Your Order, as made, gives him a right to have the sheriff seize the paintings upon posting the equivalent value into court, but deprives him of a real remedy. He simply can't afford to do so."

"I wondered when you were going to figure that out."

The judge smiled. He could see she was a fresh call to the bar. A keener. She had read the Rules of Civil Procedure and almost every case cited under the rule for interim recovery of personal property, but these were mostly commercial cases, dealing with the recovery of items of commerce such as fibreglass, doors, widgets — not original artworks by a starving artist.

The irony is that Francesca had gone into law

school because she didn't want to starve. Propelled by a writer's block, she figured if she couldn't write, at least she should do something that would burn the hours like fire to human hair, make the yearning to write impossible, staunch the flame at its source. The other irony was that most of her first clients, the files upon which she cut her baby lawyer's teeth, were starving artists who could ill afford legal services and who came to Francesca whenever they encountered legal woes because they hoped she wouldn't charge a fee.

Her artist friend, Chinkok Tan, was more established than most, not only as a professional artist, but through his paid teaching position in the fine arts department at the Ontario College of Art and Design University. Gentleman that he was, always respectful of another's work, with an immigrant's attitude to paying for what you need in life if you cannot create it yourself, not believing in debt or stiffing another human being for unpaid services, Chinkok Tan had managed to come up with a modest retainer of $3,000. But for the most part, Francesca was back to starving — this time as a lawyer.

The Judge amended his Order, deleting the requirement to post security, but required that Francesca return to him in seven days, on notice, after she and Chinkok Tan had recovered the paintings and served all respondents, including Harvey Flicker, Harvey Flicker Art Space and David Frump, the art gallery's lawyer. David Frump had some of Chinkok Tan's paintings gracing the walls of his Law Chambers, by way of his own retainer and recompense. Working his fees this way, David Frump wouldn't have to pay tax, and who knows, the artist might become really famous some day and the artwork appreciate in value. David Frump looked every part the sharp barrister and solicitor Francesca expected him to be, down to the Harry Rosen business suit, curved spine, and vulture nose.

David Frump was furious. He called Francesca's senior partner, Jack, and demanded to know who was this female pit-bull terrier Jack had working in his law firm? Jack called Francesca into his office and required an explanation. When Francesca gave it to him, Jack smiled approvingly and waved her out of his office.

"Carry on."

And so, she did. Upon the return date, the Judge remained satisfied that Chinkok Tan had established the paintings were his, on a balance of probabilities, that they had been unlawfully detained by the Art Gallery and the Art Gallery's lawyer, and that there had been a failure to remit commissions.

As Francesca waited for the Judge's ruling on costs, David Frump began drafting his Notice of Appeal, outside the motion chambers.

"Can we speak?"

"I'm busy," David Frump said.

"Surely, it's not if Harvey Flicker and Harvey Flicker Art Space owe Chinkok Tan the money, but when and how much? Don't you think your clients should make mine an offer to settle? You won't have to draft a hopeless appeal if you can get Flicker and Flicker to settle. We'll be settled, in a flicker, if you'll forgive the pun."

And settle, they did.

After that, David Frump became Francesca's best referral source.

And this is how Francesca met the wrecking ball client, George Wruck, who owned a demolition company.

"He's rough around the edges," David said, trying to warn her. The wrecking-ball client, George, had married a Russian hooker, Ivanka Shakaroff. The Russian Ivanka had snatched their baby boy and bolted to Quebec. Rough-around-the-edges George was charming in that he was hopelessly in love with Ivanka. Francesca

got an Order for return of the infant to the juris-
diction of Ontario. George and Francesca flew to
Montreal, together, for a settlement meeting and
turn-over of the child.

Before the meeting, with time to spare, knowing that George's real objective was to woo back
his Russian hooker wife, Francesca and George
went shopping together along *rue Sainte-Catherine*,
for a tie to match his new olive-green suit. Roman-
cing Ivanka would be more permanent than any
Court Order, but George Wruck wasn't just being strategic. George genuinely loved Ivanka.

Admittedly, George looked spectacular in his
new suit and tie. There's something to be said for
the unambiguous, heterosexual male. George
Wruck had the body for a fitted suit although it
was unfortunate about the missing tooth when
he smiled. He positively beamed to see Ivanka
Shakaroff and the baby in the Montreal counsel's
boardroom, but there was no denying the im-
pressiveness of his construction-worker body, now
businessman. He dominated the boardroom.
Ivanka was a stunning woman with a shapely
body, returned to its pre-birthing firmness. She
was dressed chastely for the occasion. She wore a
black tunic-like dress with a white undergarment,
unadorned, which accentuated her beautiful

body. Ivanka was her own adornment. She looked up, briefly, at George, a delicate though deliberate look. Francesca thought this was intended to communicate vulnerability, but what Francesca saw was a manipulative power.

George locked Ivanka in his sights across the boardroom table and spoke to her directly, as if she were the only person in the room.

"You know what we did to make this baby together, how we did it. This baby is mine. You're mine. Return to me what is mine."

The lawyers inhaled. Only a man rough-around-the edges could get away with saying such a thing. Ivanka just gazed at George, then abruptly asked both counsels to leave the room. Half an hour later, Ivanka and George emerged from the boardroom, together, and left the office, swinging the baby car seat, between them.

George told Francesca afterward that Ivanka had jumped his bones in the boardroom with their kid asleep under the boardroom table.

Francesca thought it was strategic on Ivanka's part. Ivanka likely realized, with the benefit of Montreal counsel, she had no property entitlements in Quebec. She'd do much better in Ontario where she could sue for an equalization which would include George's business. For years

Ivanka played these drama games with George, until she drove him out of business, then left him for a richer man who owned his own companies, had a second child, eventually a third—all by a succession of very rich fathers.

But it felt great for that one day. It was a great thing to see a man get the return of that which belonged to him, what he had created himself, to have played a part in that brief replevin.

Years later, Francesca and her husband, Zachary, vacationing in St. Andrews By-The-Sea, during their first summer of marriage, crossed paths on a local street with Chinkok Tan who was teaching a summer art course. But Zachary had to abort their holiday, peremptorily, upon receiving a phone call from his secretary. The other lawyers sharing chambers with him were moving out, taking their files along with the brass light fixtures and brass electrical plates, which the secretary knew Zachary had purchased. The secretary was hysterical. She didn't know what was happening nor what to do, and the lawyers wouldn't answer her questions. Zachary had to get back to take care of business. He urged Francesca to stay behind in St. Andrews By-The-Sea and enjoy the balance of her holiday. Francesca had worked so hard for it. She owed herself this holiday.

Chinkok Tan invited Francesca to take the art course with him, but Francesca was too riddled with anxiety to take him up on the offer. She did, however, spend a day with him, watching him paint. In the field where he painted, with its lonely dark tree on the hill, Chin (as she had taken to calling him) pointed out the wild peas growing there. Francesca picked the peas and shelled them for the meal she would later make for Chin and herself—a bouillabaisse of shrimp and scallops. While normally Francesca would make a linguine to go with the bouillabaisse, the rice and peas upon which she served up the seafood were her gift to Chin. Using the modest resources of her facility cabin, the garlic and tomatoes she was able to purchase in town, she invited Chin to her impromptu dinner. Together, Francesca and Chin sat out on the picnic table outside her facility cabin, overlooking the sea. That night, after Francesca had cleaned up the dishes, she went outside again, alone, and listened to the sound of a piper walking the length of the wharf, piping the soulful spiritual "Amazing Grace." A thick fog rolled in. When Francesca went inside to write her letter to Zachary, her clothes were wet from the fog.

Zachary, my sweet husband,

St. Andrews By-The-Sea is so very quiet. I can hear myself for the first time in so long. I feel like I have returned to myself, here. I have tried to reach you many times by phone, last night and this morning, and again this evening. My little galavanter. I have been missing you very much.

Today I visited an old graveyard and read some of the fascinating stones. It is almost comforting, the way the dead are buried together: young women and their cousins; fathers and infant sons, all remembered on a single stone. (I am returning tomorrow to record an inscription that particularly touched me.) I went swimming in the heated pool at that beautiful Lodge on the hill. After that I read my book on the lawn chairs, where we saw the man and woman at shuffleboard. A fog had rolled in while I read *Love and Shadows*, the fog so dense that I noticed the page was covered in dew. I went to the antique shop and antiquarian bookshop across from the Lodge. The old books were just fascinating.

There was one called *A Writer's Holiday*, where the writer explains to his readers why, despite pleas for his books, he took a holiday even after being acquitted of the libel suit in which he had been involved. I had never heard of the writer, but from the introduction he seemed to have an enormous popular following, according to his own self-description. Then there was *The Lady's Book*—a complete manual to being a woman, replete with coloured plates showing "the four stages of life:" Baptism, Girlhood, Marriage, and Death. Judging by the gravestones in the cemetery —the 20-year-olds, the 30-something woman buried with her infant child, I suppose that really was the sequence of existence. Although there were some who lived to be ripe 86-year-olds. I flipped through old *LIFE* magazines and read an interesting article on Fra Angelico, an artist whose work I studied my summer in Florence before starting practice.

The fog was very dense as I walked back. I got in completely chilled and had a late afternoon "nip." After an early dinner at 6 o'clock, I fell fast asleep. The sea air makes me very sleepy, and I have had the deepest nights here. I don't want to uncurl in the morning.

I have missed you so much, Zachary. Today, I even wished that I had returned with you. I miss snuggling up to you at night, your soft warmth. I miss everything about you. I truly love being with you, Zachary. I so look forward to going to bed with you at night. It is my favourite part of the day when you fold me in your arms and throw a leg across mine. I miss the soft tickle of your beard, the devil in your brown eyes.

My sweet love, we have been so very lucky to have found each other.

Zachary, I wish you luck with what is going down at the office and the planning of your future. Call me if you wish to discuss anything before I return. Take care of our pretty home (check burners, lock our doors). Take care of my sweet love, remember to eat properly. Think of me when you break bread before you fall to sleep at night. I'll think of you then, especially, too.

Love,
Your wife, Francesca

She had loved calling herself "your wife," had loved calling Zachary "my husband," though it lasted less than a decade. Her senior partner, Jack, with his acute understanding of human nature, told Francesca that as long as she was married to Zachary, she'd always be plugging her fingers into the dike, until one day she would run out of fingers.

Oddly, in all her letters to Zachary from St. Andrews By-The-Sea, she never once mentioned making dinner for Chin nor watching him paint, nor listening to the lone piper playing "Amazing Grace."

But she did eventually buy the painting she had watched Chinkok Tan make over the course of that week — for $3,000. For the longest time, Chin's painting dominated the wall of her office, and when her marriage to Zachary ended, she brought it home. Whenever she looks at it now, she thinks how she had identified with the dark tree, standing alone at the crest of the hill in a descending field of bright lupins. How ironic that she had thought herself returned to herself in that little town by the sea, that she had thought herself able to hear her own voice, again for the first time in so long. St. Andrews By-The-Sea. Her personal replevin.

The thing about the replevied goods — they

never come back the same. Chinkok Tan burned the paintings Flicker and Frump had tried to steal from him; he burned these works to create space in his studio for the works he was yet to create. Francesca's worry about the burners and the unlocked doors proved prophetic as the pretty little home she and Zachary had owned together went up in proverbial smoke. It was lost to his creditors who would pursue her for years, long after the marriage ended. Zachary continued to give out her phone number so long as it deflected attention away from himself. That's the thing about replevied goods — the damage done is never repaired, the losses never fully recovered.

Borrowed Babies

A baby cries unrelentingly in their section of the airplane, distressing everyone within earshot. Why wasn't the mother doing something to calm it? For Francesca who had given birth only 10 months earlier, her own baby recently weaned, her response was physical: she needed to feed this child.

"Please," she said, having made her way up the aisle, just after the cabin lights dimmed, "I am missing my baby. Could I feed yours?"

The real mother paused in conversation with her female travelling companion.

"I don't have enough formula to last to Ireland."

"I'm sure the airline will supply some. I am so far from my baby," she said, careful not to sound accusatory, but to put it in terms of her own need.

"Oh, very well." The mother, impatient, searched about her bag, and pulled out a bottle.

Francesca lifted the crying child from the

airline bassinette and sat in the empty seat beside the mother who resumed her conversation wholly disengaged from the child. Francesca tucked the babe securely close to her own breast as she had seen her own mother do, as she herself had done, cradled in the crook of her right arm, his left hand dangling beside her, right hand clasping her blouse, his small face planted against her breast. She touched the plastic nipple to his lower lip, and his small mouth instantly attached. Cries stopped, replaced by a greedy suckling. The babe opened his eyes wide and looked at her, as if astonished, then closed his eyes again.

Francesca studied his face, his crown of red hair, the closed baby-bird eyes with their blue veins, the movement beneath the lids. Six weeks of age, she judged. He did not appear to be thriving. Poor little thing. She doesn't love you, does she? It's all right. You keep crying. Someone will respond. She overheard the women, talking to her left, as if she, just as this baby boy, didn't exist. From snatches of their conversation, she understood the mother to be leaving the boy's father. The child looked nothing like his mother, so she assumed he must look like his dad. Perhaps his mother hated him on this account or, at minimum, was indifferent to him. Half the bottle done, Francesca transferred the babe to her other arm, the way she'd done with her own when she breastfed. Now his right arm dangled as his left fist reached up toward her face, his cheek tucked against her swollen left breast, which was now leaking milk. Francesca had weaned her own son some months ago, but unaccountably, now, she was again leaking.

Her own boy back in Canada, in the care of her mother, was raging with a fever. She didn't know that at the time. She had no choice about the law firm's meeting in England. She had missed the last firm trip to Nassau, then being too close to her due date. Her husband had wanted to go without her. She in fact had gone into labour just as all the lawyers returned. "What, are we in labour?" one of the partners had asked her as he saw her leave at four o'clock, that afternoon. "As a matter of fact, Bill," she'd said, "we are." Tough litigator though he was, Bill coloured a deep crimson. Francesca hadn't wanted to go to England for this year's firm meeting, hadn't wanted this separation from her son. She was clinging to her work, to the wreckage of her marriage. She had to keep her job at the firm.

The feeding done, she raised the babe gently, supporting his chin with her right hand and rubbed his little back gently until he burped. She rocked him to sleep. Then she laid him back in his airline manger, folded the blankets around him and kissed his forehead.

"Thank you," she said to the mother, who looked back, startled, as if she'd completely forgotten about them both.

As Francesca returned to her seat in her own darkened section of the airplane, a relieved stranger, hoping for sleep, reached out and caught her arm.

"Thank you," he said.

Years later, a male law partner (they had all been travelling together on the same flight for the firm's annual meeting) would laugh about this junior lawyer who brought her baby and Nanny along for the England trip.

"Oh, no," Francesca had said, horrified, "that wasn't my child."

"Then whose baby was it?"

"God only knows …"

She often wondered about that baby, what became of him, and the gift of indifference that enabled her to borrow the child for a single feeding.

Château Cuisine

Whatever propels her to *Château Cuisine* is as mysterious as where and how she came by the book. The pheasants were a gift from a man who ate nothing he himself did not kill or forage, like the *chanterelles* that would accompany them. Preparation of the pheasants will occur New Year's Day, in honour of the new life she is determined to create—hence the need for a new and challenging recipe. And who better to do game than the French? So, casting about in her recipe books, Francesca finds the promising title of *Château Cuisine*—*et voilà*! *Faisan à la Massena* (roast pheasant stuffed with *chanterelles* and oyster mushrooms); *faisans en escabèche* (oil and vinegar braised pheasants in aspic); and *faisans à la Chartreuse* (pheasants *en cocotte* with Chartreuse liqueur)—the three possibilities the text offers, in sumptuous tribute to a heritage of castle architecture and rich taste.

In celebration, Francesca pours herself another large glass of the Crystal Head Vodka a grateful client has given her this Christmas and looks at the university-aged man-child sprawled on her couch—home for the holidays, asleep with the excesses of exams, Christmas, and alcohol. Her one, only son. They were supposed to put up the last of the Christmas tree decorations together—photos of her son's Christmases past, 22 in total, including the one where Francesca is pregnant with him, standing in front of their first Christmas tree—but he crashed on the couch immediately after dinner.

So, Francesca put up these decorations alone. Some of the photographs included his father; she didn't think it fair to exclude these. She plugged in the lights and stood back to survey her creation. Laden with the weight of time, this year's Christmas tree is spectacular.

Feeling suddenly cold, although in front of the fireplace, she draws the Christmas throw more tightly about herself, and tucks back into her book of *Château Cuisine*, to learn about "trussing a bird" with needle and string in the glossary of explanations. Mentally removing the powdered gelatine from the recipe for *faisans en escabèche*, and replacing it with the four small firm apples, peeled, cored, thickly sliced into rings and halved, to be flamed with four tablespoons of Armagnac from the recipe for *faisans à la Massena*, she thinks of adding the wild mushrooms to the already prepared stuffing in her refrigerator of fresh walnuts, seasoned breadcrumbs, carrots, and finely sliced fennel (to add her own personal, Sicilian touch) to her New Year's creation. She wonders what is upsetting her, what dark presence squats at the corner of her mind, a gargoyle on the buttresses of her imagination, when she turns the pages to the source of the book:

Good memories … the start of many more

David & Olga
Christmas, 1992

And there it is—the *Château du Marais*, where she and her then toddler and husband stayed for two weeks with David and Olga, new acquaintances from her son's "stay-and-play." Her husband, Zachary, had suggested she invite them on this holiday with his Scottish frugality (only generous when someone else was footing the bill) not wishing to waste anything when future profit might be in the balance, not least of all the five rooms with en-suite bathrooms in their wing of the *Château du Marais*. He invited them on impulse (his recipe for living), although they barely knew David and Olga, and their child Alessandra. Francesca herself had sublet the wing from her senior partner, Jack, with another partner to follow upon their departure. The real generosity belonged to Jack, who had suggested it in the first place, using two weeks of his four, as he had tired of the *Château du Marais* as Jack tired of most everything, including his over-zealous junior.

"You take the law too seriously. You need to lighten up, have some fun. Go to France with that husband of yours. Take a few friends."

How to explain that she was working too hard as his junior to have any friends. David and she had met early Saturday mornings, watching their respective children (her Marco, David's Alessandra) play alongside each other in the church basement, while their respective spouses slept late. They quickly discovered something in common, apart from having children the same age: they were both "morning people" — their personal hearts-of-darkness tending to come in the early afternoons. Francesca liked the fact that David shaved his face and was the only father not in jogging pants. He actually came to these Saturday mornings respectably dressed.

And there it is, too — the artificial lake, over 500 metres long where Francesca had rowed the little boat for her son, and where a small plane had flown over and landed, Francesca frantically pointing their little craft to meet the swell — the artificial lake, normally so still, reflecting all it sees, such that it is known as "the mirror," says the text, and the grounds of which, rich in escargot, have been strolled by the likes of Chateaubriand and Madame de Staël:

> Under the American duchess, the *Château du Marais* again became an exclusive haven for Europe's nobility: her granddaughter, known as the Duchesse de Sagan, is the present owner. She shares with her three children the task of maintaining the *Château* and its outbuildings, which include an orangery, a museum devoted to family history and a functioning water mill, besides 25 hectares of parkland. 'It is so hard to preserve,' laments Comtesse Guy de Bagneux, the Duchesse's daughter.

'We are only 40 kilometres from Paris. Highways and power lines encroach all the time.' For Comtesse Guy the menace seems all the more threatening—her most nostalgic childhood memories are of intimate afternoon tea in the park with her legendary American grandmother. 'The chef prepared special cakes, but what we all loved best was cinnamon toast.'

And in the kitchen that is part of their "wing" Francesca prepares *tortellini in brodo*, using fresh thyme, rosemary and parsley from the *Château's* gardens, for her one, only son, Olga and David, and her husband, of course. She and Zachary shop at the local marketplaces every morning; he convinces her to try unique foods, including horse. She makes *cheval à la cacciatore* from a recipe she carries in her head, along with *fricassée de lapin aux trois racines* (rabbit stew with root vegetables), for the less adventurous. Together, the two couples drink wine copiously while Olga and David's child eats only wieners and coloured Cheerios. And at the open window, during mealtimes, David sits guard, with his long legs, making sure that neither child falls to his or her death on the terraces below.

She discovers something in common with Olga. One day, as Francesca is deboning the boiled chicken, Olga asks: "What are you going to do with that?" She speaks of the gristle at the tail of the breastbone.

"Oh, I always eat it, my little secret in the kitchen. It's my favourite part of the chicken — my peasant roots!"

"Then I have them, too, because it's my favourite part of the chicken."

With the next chicken she prepares, Francesca serves up the gristle to Olga, on the chipped Limoges discovered amid the saucers of their kitchen cupboard. Olga laughs as she removes the paper napkin, to discover this gift, Francesca's little sacrifice to their new friendship.

And yes, they are all part of the plan — of preservation — the paying tourists, without whom the Duchesse could not keep up the place, but whose presence is a barely tolerated encroachment, which, in the case of Francesca, becomes intolerable, after all. Is it because the Duchesse expected them to behave like *paysans*?

And try as Francesca might — to leave no footprint, as if they had never been — with Olga's help — Olga, of the Polish cleaning-lady origins — it was not to be. The Duchesse would never visit their apartments, in any event, never see for herself, how spotless they had kept their rooms, until after their departure, after the disaster, and would refuse to "receive" any one of Francesca's phone calls of entreaty.

So Francesca never got to lay the apology, nor reparations at the Duchesse's feet. Instead, the Duchesse simply confiscated their American funds, the funds Francesca had brought for the entire month, and simply bolted the doors to the other partner, who arrived the next day, fully unaware of what had happened, his entry and that of his guests equally barred.

No intercession on the part of the senior partner, Jack, could avail. Guest though Jack had been for the past four summers, his bicycles and Cuisinart now likewise seized in her turrets, the Duchesse would not take his second call.

"She accused you of doing crude things in her forest. I know that is not you. I know you are a lady of Loretto, would not permit your son to defecate in her woods, nor you ever do that yourself."

It was not simply a question of the mirror …

"I did not come all this way to spend every day beside a pool," Francesca complains to her husband.

"I'm content with just this. Why can't you be? Why can't you just relax?"

"We're only 40 minutes from Paris. Can't we at least hop a train? Marco travels well. He'll be happy anywhere we are."

She had a Mothercraft portable potty. There would be no regression, for Francesca's son, as with Alessandra, whose parents had returned her to diapers for this trip.

"I have the perfect suggestion for what ails you."

"Nothing ails me," Francesca said, lying, for in fact, her panic attacks had begun again in the night, and then chased her as she tried to work them off, jogging about the grounds ...

"Lower your expectations ..."

Diminished expectations had been what marrying Zachary was all about—an unbearable loneliness of being, that she would never meet the man who would cherish her for who she was, that he, after all, was at least easy to be with, or so it had seemed, at the time. She hadn't foreseen how arduous it could be to claw one's way out of a collapsing house, to constantly be picking through salvage for the necessities of life, what was left after the latest storm, the latest lawsuit, like the one she had most recently defended before departing for France. They had moved house, ten days before this holiday, and she'd sat 10 Hamiltons (her husband's people) down to dinner, the day before travel — roast-beef and Yorkshire-pudding — a feast spread out on the harvest table with the bone china she and the Nanny had washed before the move, a feast which she had been unable to eat. Only she knew of the injunctive order that her senior partner had negotiated to be lifted, briefly, to enable the two real estate closings, before being transferred to Francesca's new home. Like a stain on the white lace table-cloth — this cloud against her title. It meant she could not sell or even finance, without having to deal with her husband's creditors.

Her son slept in the sumptuous room off the *Château*'s dining room, separated from theirs by a long corridor that would have befitted a boudoir farce. Nightly, she settled Marco and read him to sleep, until she heard his gentle breathing, while David and Zachary conversed, and Olga did the dishes, as Francesca had cooked the meal. Then Francesca would slip out of bed, and down the inner corridor that divided their rooms from the outer hallway that dissected the suites on opposite sides of the *Château*. Olga and David's rooms faced the mirror lake; Francesca and Zachary's looked out upon the gardens. She would lie still, listening to the voices of David and her husband that carried from the open window of the dining room to her open window ... and wait.

What courage did it take this toddler son — to face the length of that corridor, alone? Nightly she would find relief in the sound of Marco's little feet hitting the floor from the high perch of his canopied bed, running wordlessly down the corridor toward their room, where, in silent choreography, his father would scoop him up and deposit him into Francesca's open arms, then retreat to the other room, where father could better sleep out the night into the late mornings, uninterrupted, while Francesca and son would take their little boat on the mirror lake, or sit together in the swings, with inarticulate loneliness, at dawn.

On one of these walks, far away from the *Château*, Marco announced that he had to go poo-poo, and Francesca, looking around, walked with him deeper into the woods, found a low-hanging branch, looked around to ensure that no one was about, and removed the portable Mother-craft potty from her knapsack—proud of her own resourcefulness.

That afternoon, as every afternoon, they all congregated at the pool, David's Olga and Francesca's husband finally emerged from their sleep, Francesca and David ready for their first glass of wine—"tonic" as David called it, to chase the afternoon's heart-of-darkness.

"Paris is only 40 kilometres from here. Can't we at least go to Paris?"

And so, to try to placate her restlessness, Francesca's husband suggested a drive. And sometimes, motion did help.

In the back seat, beside her son, Francesca looks out at the countryside, the long avenues of regal trees, alternating with farmlands, little villages. After hours of driving, it all begins to look alike.

"Where are we going?"

"Leave it to me; it's a surprise. Do you have to control everything?"

So, Francesca sits back and sings to her son. Eventually, they arrive.

It is an outdoor restaurant, in the middle of nowhere. They are the only patrons of the place. Francesca is charmed. They sit under the mature trees at a metal table. The owner spreads a cloth, as her husband orders a rich burgundy, assorted cheeses and fruits. The proprietor returns to their table with a tiered platter, compliments of the chef, its three layers flowering with shrimp, little snails, and assorted seafood — no doubt about to go bad. Seeing the lavish display, Marco bursts into song: "Happy Birthday to you …" They all laugh. It is indeed an occasion. Francesca claps her hands together, as does her son. She is suddenly, deliriously happy, abandoned at this exquisite moment, the unexpected gift of this afternoon.

"Are you all right to drive?" Francesca asks Zachary.

"We haven't far to go."

He pulls out of the restaurant parking lot, round one corner, and they are there, at the locked gates of the *Château du Marais*. He laughs at her realization, the dismay on her face. They have driven around in circles, only to land right back at the gates of the *Château*. He has managed to deceive her, yet again. His laughter, like the one the morning after their wedding, when at breakfast, he had lit a cigarette. Fool that she was, she believed him when he told her he had quit smoking. Or the day after their return from Jamaica, when she found the marijuana he had smuggled across the border — no *souciance* for the potential implications for his license to practice law, his wife, or their son ... Laughing at the fish hook in her cheek, her "trout look," as he is fond of calling it.

The eyes and ears of the Duchesse must have been everywhere. How else could the Duchesse know that Olga had purchased fireworks to celebrate "Bastille Day?" How else could she know about the defecation in her woods?

The fireworks were to be David and Olga's gift to them for this holiday — a night's entertainment to be viewed from the open window of the dining room after dark.

One of the Duchesse's servants arrived at the door of their apartments: "Here, at the *Château*, we do not celebrate Bastille Day. Here, at the *Château*, there will be no fireworks."

The property quickly passed from *Le Maître* to a young widow. Madame de la Briche, who organised country festivals for the peasantry. 'We set large tables in the parkland alleys,' she recorded in her diary. 'The only expenses for a charming day, full of gaiety and goodwill, were the cakes and spice breads, the wine, and the violinists for dancing.' Her generosity was happily rewarded, for *Le Marais* was left untouched during the Revolution.

≈

It was not simply a question of the mirror.

≈

Francesca is cleaning their apartments, using the vacuum cleaner Olga has located in a servant's cupboard. The cord is extended the length of their bedroom, as Francesca works toward the master bathroom, and is in front of the full-view, stand-up and adjustable mirror, when her son bursts into the bedroom with his father, his arms extended toward her, little legs pumping. Francesca watches, as if in slow motion, at the obstacles between herself and the child; she tries to swing the cord in her left hand like a whip, away from his pumping feet, just as his left foot hooks the cord and hurtles him forward, a flailing Icarus, flying with his hands outreached toward the mirror. Francesca hurls herself toward her son and catches him, in midair, but not before his little hands contact the mirror and send it hurtling backward, toward the tiled floor of the bathroom. From where they roll on the carpet, her arms and body shielding him, she looks up in time to see the disaster as it unfolds — impact of the wood frame, the bounce, the shattering of the antique mirror into a thousand pieces.

The collateral shatterings to follow:

The business David founded, stolen by his partner while they were away in France.

David's oppression lawsuit, which will eventually bankrupt David and Olga, beginning with the collapse of their retirement funds.

Zachary's bankruptcy.

Then Zachary's suspension by the Law Society.

Their marital separation, when their son is only six.

David and Olga's home — lost to the Trustee in bankruptcy when David and Olga become unable to pay their debts as these become due. (Only the contents survive, whisked into some relative's barn, to be hidden under straw.)

The old Pontiac Sunbird that Francesca lets David and Olga use, then needs, herself, for her own salvage operations.

"I'm sorry, Olga. I'm so sorry. He's not giving me any child support. You can either pay me or give it back, so I can sell it elsewhere."

Olga sends David with the money.

At the hand-over meeting Francesca says: "You know, he's got a woman—already."

"You mean the Brenda woman?" David says.

Until that moment, Francesca had only suspected. The name registers like a slap.

"I'm so sorry," David says, when he sees the impact.

The sale of the old Pontiac to David and Olga saved her a few weeks of groceries. It cost Francesca their friendship.

Good memories? Such had been their denials and delusions at the time that, years later, she has blocked out even the fact of this book and how it came to be in her library.

Francesca gets up quietly before the fireplace of the house she has managed to salvage. She gets up quietly—lest she waken the sleeping son who is moving from boy to man even as he sleeps, moving out of her protection. She goes to search her cabinets for Armagnac with which to marinate the cavities of her pheasants to be flamed with cored, peeled, and thickly sliced apples.

While she is in the kitchen, the Christmas tree pitches forward—a matter simply of timing and the unbalanced weight of decorations. She listens frozen, with her hand on the kitchen cabinet, to the sound of shattering.

They collide just outside the door to the kitchen. She blocks her son's bound into the front room with his size 10 bare feet. Shattered bulbs are everywhere. They stand, surveying the wreckage. Water bleeds from the base of the tree and across the surface of the hardwood. A photograph floats free in the river toward her.

It is of herself—standing pregnant and waiting in front of their first Christmas tree. She picks it up. Her eyes stare into her eyes—across 21 years. It was there all the time. Even this. Nothing to do with the mirror, his future or her own.

"Does your Dad ever talk about the time we stayed in a castle?"

"Dad never mentions the past."

"I found a recipe for pheasant while you were sleeping. I'm making pheasants New Year's Day."

"Cool."

"We stayed in a castle, with David and Olga. They had this little girl, Alessandra. She loved to kiss you under the table. We were always finding the two of you embracing. Do you remember any of it?

"I remember a bat. You hid under the blankets with me until Dad chased it away. You were really afraid."

"I forgot about the bat. I was that ... afraid."

"Dad asked me once if you still kept in touch with them. I told him 'no.' He said that was a shame."

The apples will have a sweet, peppery taste. The recipe will turn out well in the end. Strong, peasant roots that she has, Francesca always ensures they eat well. Anyway, it is not about the food, but the company. Francesca may not have kept in touch, but she thinks of Olga every time she eats the gristle, which is every time she makes chicken soup, and of David whenever she sees a Pontiac Sunbird. They are there, just as she is, in every mirror.

Travel Talismans

"If you care about us, you will plan a holiday, book it, and pay for it," Francesca tells her husband, Zachary.

The "pay for it" is particularly important as Francesca is exhausted with overwork, with plugging her fingers in the dike of her husband's financial risk-taking and creditors.

She buys Jamaican roti and beer at the airport for the hour-long bus ride to the resort. She swims deliriously in the unexpected lightness of salt and sun. While their son, Marco, sleeps, she demonstrates her gratitude to her husband for this trip. Zachary did this for her, for their son! It isn't until sometime later she will realize Zachary has decided on bankruptcy. He never will pay for this holiday.

After dinner, the stabbing pains begin across the top of her stomach. Zachary is having a fine time with the other tourists, especially the ones from Canada. He is particularly taken with the "work ethic" of Vee-may, who has just had a baby, he informs her, who is a dental hygienist from Brampton, Ontario, and who has paid for this trip for her family. After dinner, Vee-may and Zachary have a dance, poolside. Feeling awkward for herself and Vee-may's husband, Francesca invites Vee-may's husband to dance. But she must excuse herself from the dancefloor, abruptly, as her cramps develop into something more serious. By midnight, Francesca thinks she will die.

In the pitch black of night, the Jamaican man arrives at their door in what looks like maintenance clothing, having responded to her phone call to the hotel operator. He is enormous, a Rastafarian with lengthy dreadlocks; he stands about 6'4" — in contrast to her own 5'2" diminutive frame, though her clients always tell her she appears large in the courtroom and are surprised when she stands up behind her desk. Francesca is too ill to be afraid, too considerate to call for Zachary who snores relentlessly in his sleep. Wordless, the Jamaican Rastafarian holds out a large spoon that he fills with thick white liquid from a bottle. Fevered and limp in her white nightgown, Francesca opens her mouth obediently and drinks what the stranger offers, only afterward asking: "What was it?"

"Gravol." He hands her little white pills in a package and tells her to take two every three hours until the vomiting and diarrhea stop.

For days afterward, Francesca lies on her rack-of-a bed in the darkened room, sipping tea and listening to the waves thudding against the shore. Her husband will bring Marco back to her every afternoon, slipping him down beside her for his nap. Her little boy's arms grow up around her neck, and she embraces his salty body with hungry gratitude, clinging to him as to a raft.

Only after the pictures are developed will she learn of her boy's adventures — at Dunn's River Falls, holding onto his father under a curtain of water, closed eyes and screaming mouth under pouring water. Then, at the plantation, sucking on sugar cane; then poolside, a helium balloon tied to the freshly beaded curl at the back of his head so his lolling father could keep track of him without moving from his deck chair. What parent would risk losing their child with nothing more protective than a helium balloon tied to a curl? Francesca, Zachary has told her, is too "uptight" in her parenting, having to keep track of their son every moment. But Francesca has been too ill to keep track of anything, even the time.

On the third day, she emerges briefly with her laptop from the darkness of the room onto the patio. The hospitality guide giving a tour sweeps a hand in her direction: "And then there are those who can never relax, not even in paradise." Francesca listens as the laughter fades, like the voices that drift in and out of her louvered windows. These make horizontal bars on the wall beside her bed, which she sometimes traces with her fingers, as she moves between dreams, listening to the waves, counting out the seconds between thuds as they fall to shore.

On the fourth day, she meets the fellow tourists her gregarious husband has befriended, including the woman Zachary will eventually bed. Francesca learns Vee-may's newborn is back at home in Brampton with Vee-may's mother. Francesca can't imagine ever leaving her newborn with anyone, but perhaps it is different if you are on your third child. Francesca never got beyond Marco. When Marco asked her why he never had any siblings, she tells her son that she couldn't imagine loving another child as much as he.

Francesca remembers only one afternoon, spent ocean-side, together. There is a single photo of Francesca and her husband, taken by their four-year-old son: Francesca and Zachary lean down and forward into the camera with concerned faces, wondering if they will both make it into the same frame. Their four-year-old son holds them together, by the lens of the camera.

On the last night, Zachary insists they all eat with Vee-may and her family, though Francesca had hoped to have this night alone with Zachary, their own little family, so needing to heal, so needing to find again whatever it was that had prompted Francesca and Zachary to marry, to have a child. Vee-may walks in a queenly fashion ahead of their group, taking a hand from each of her sons; her ass sways provocatively for the sake of those at her rear. Vee-may makes a sudden pivot to the left, plunging directly into the pool, fully clothed, taking each of her boys with her before either knows what has happened. The youngest surfaces, as does his mother, choking with laughter, but the eldest howls between outraged gasps, his arms flailing. This one will sulk into the next day of departure, warily sitting apart from his mother, even at the airport. Francesca's husband will love Vee-may's spontaneity, of course, wanting to dive in after her. Zachary is a man who gets taken by every wind that blows; he will go to Vee-may the first Christmas of the separation, taking Marco with him for the holiday — Vee-may being able to offer the boy what Francesca never can — according to Zachary: siblings and a real sense of family. Marco will eventually refer to Vee-may's children as his "stepbrothers."

For now, Francesca contemplates the trust of travellers—in the talismans of passports, mothers, and spoons.

Blind Trust

A trust in which a settlor reserves the right to terminate the trust but to assert no other power over the trust.
— (Legal Dictionary)

#1 The Window

"**I** wouldn't trust that, if I were you." The guest beside me at the cocktail reception leaned against the security railing. On the other side, only a six-foot drop, but one that, if the railing gave way, could do considerable damage. And suddenly, my drop into memory from the end of my legal career — to the trauma of being witness to something that happened when I was about to become an articling student.

I was there — there in the boardroom where students were being wooed with cocktails on the 52nd floor of a downtown Toronto Bank tower.

Cocktail parties in the Bank tower law firms were occasions where students, good-looking on paper, could show off their social wares and articling committees got to see who did and didn't fit into the culture of their firm.

A partner with too many cocktails under his belt, three-sheets-to-the-wind, leapt onto the ledge to demonstrate his articling party trick. He hurled himself, shoulder first, with blind trust against the window. But this time was different! Caught by the wind, the window flew out like a sheet of ice and disappeared with the suited lawyer, his jacket and tie fluttering. The glass didn't shatter until it hit the ground, 52 stories below.

Those nearest the hole of the gaping window were sucked toward the void, but dropped to all fours and crawled without dignity toward the boardroom door. No one screamed. Only the wind made its whooshing sound.

The firm offered grief counselling.

#2. The Haunted House

On the other side of fear lays freedom.
—Anonymous

The opposite of fear is trust.
—Mary Walkin Keane

It started off tamely enough — the usual automated Frankenstein's monster dummy lunging forward mechanically, taped screams, and sudden illuminations behind glass to prevent tampering with the exhibits, a severed head, and walking through darkness into the sensation of hair, as if through a car wash. I held my son's hand. He took it all in, in silence, but I could tell it was nothing he couldn't handle. There was always that little warning puff as we stepped onto a part of the mat leading our way that indicated something was about to happen.

Then we came to a doorway. A narrow chamber to be entered alone. I couldn't see beyond. A step forward into the darkness before placing the foot down, feeling into the darkness, and then, stepping back. A voice. This was different. Not automated. The voice was real.

"Take my hand."

"Tell me what you're going to do, what happens, next?" I could hear outside; I knew we were close to the exit. This had to be the final attempt to terrify.

"What's there?"

"Take my hand." A white glove reached out of a curtain. But something had softened in the voice, hearing the real fear in mine. He didn't want me to worry. For whatever reason, he couldn't say this.

"Look, I know you're some university kid, earning his tuition, but I'm here with my child. I need to know what you're going to do."

I could hear the hesitation in his silence. Clearly, the voice had never encountered anything like this. A negotiation, after the entrance fee had been paid.

"Take my hand." The voice was trying to find its way back into the role.

"What happens afterward?"

I knew it couldn't be life threatening, nothing for which the Haunted House could be sued.

"Take my hand. You first."

"You think I'm going to leave my son alone in the dark?"

Another pause. Then, a whisper.

"Look, lady, there are people in line behind you. I'm just doing my job."

"Tell me what you are going to do. What's the big scare?"

"It's nothing bad."

"Then, tell me."

He wouldn't say. What kind of code of ethics bound the voice, after he'd stepped out of role?

"We're going back."

"You can't do that."

"Says who? Back, I know the way."

"This is the only way to the exit." Then back to role. "Take my hand."

"I said, no. Not unless you tell me what you're going to do with it, with me."

Silence. The voice was weighing the options.

Feeling a restlessness behind me, we stepped aside, letting the ones behind us pass through.

"Take my hand."

Screams. Of course. With the third scream, I terminated the trust and exited by the front door, son safely in hand.

The Magna Carta

"What are they doing?" There were no flashing lights on the cop car, but Francesca figured if she pulled into the intersection in front of it, the cops would haul her over for some infraction. So, she and her son, Marco, waited patiently in front of St. Michael's Cathedral at the intersection of Bond and Shuter Streets, behind the cop car chuffing exhaust in a wintry idle. Finally, Francesca put her car in park, flicked on the hazards and got out.

"No, Ma, don't."

Ignoring her son's street smarts, she went up to the window, tapped twice, and asked, as politely as possible.

"Officers, are you going through? Right? Left? What are you doing?"

"Get back in your car, ma'am," the cop said, equally polite.

Obediently, she got back in the car and watched

as the big cop got out of the driver's seat. He adjusted his pants by the buckle as he walked toward her window and tapped twice, signalling her to open. With the double tap to her window, she wondered if he was mimicking her. His face was flat and pink, his pale-blue eyes almost dead looking. She couldn't read him.

"Put on your windshield wipers, ma'am," he requested. She complied, then watched as the wipers swished back and forth. She looked up at the cop, confused.

"There, now. Can you see any better?"

A whoosh of rage blossomed behind her eyes. Now she knew with certainty he was making fun of her in front of her ten-year-old son, as if she were stupid.

"You ever heard of the Magna Carta, officer? The law exists for me and you. You're idling at an intersection, without signalling. Signals are meant to inform other drivers what you're going to do so they can act accordingly. I can't tell if you're going forward, right, left through the intersection or parking. And this, by the way, is a no-standing zone. See that sign? You're not above the law, officer, and you're lucky I don't ask for your badge number, which by law you'd be obliged to give to me." She looked into his flat face and smiled.

He remained silent during her tirade, his eyes

widening only slightly at mention of the Magna Carta, and she felt like a schoolteacher scolding a pupil, not the lawyer nor the partner of a downtown law firm dressing down another officer of the law.

He turned and walked back to the cop car. Francesca could almost see the slow burn of a brain, searching his fifth-grade history book, wordlessly, when her son said: "Fuck, Mom, the Magna Carta?"

"Dial it back, young man. Mr. Sorbie said you curse like a drunken sailor."

Then the cop car signalled right, and slowly made a right turn onto Shuter Street.

Mother and son burst out laughing. She was glad she hadn't just let it go. Every step they took together was a shared lesson. No one is above the law. Not a cop. Not a king.

She had a sick feeling in her stomach.

... Playing blocks, at the age of four. Her mother had been ironing to CFRB on the radio, with its soothing and familiar music. But when the voices came, these sounded frightened. Something bad was happening. The blocks with which she played were the facings of a church, or maybe a courthouse, she now thinks. She never thought of the blocks as making a house in which people could live. Some blocks had painted columns. Without sides, it was sure the blocks would fall. Still, over and over again, she placed the blocks on top of one another, to match the picture on the box, with the triangle roof on top.

It wasn't the tumble of the blocks that gave her that sick feeling, but the word "nuclear." On the radio news, the President had given an "ultimatum" to a man named Castro. "Ultimatum" became her new word of the week. She loved big words. She especially loved the way the eyes of adults widened, whenever she used them. But this word gave her a sick feeling.

"Are we all going to die, Momma?"

"Of course not," her mother had said, without pausing in her ironing.

But she knew her dad had built a bomb shelter in the furnace room, saw it stocked with bottled water and Spam, and other tinned foods they didn't eat regularly. They had bomb shelter drills, but never practiced sleeping there. She didn't want to live if it meant living days in the basement. Even at the age of four, she had thought about that.

That sick feeling in her stomach.

Francesca knew about her husband's creditors. What she didn't know was how close these creditors were to banging down the front door. She suggested that she and Zachary take Marco down to Sunnyside on Lake Ontario, after dinner, to the dinosaur park. While their son played on a seesaw and swings, she and Zackary could talk.

Adults think kids don't hear, don't understand words like "ultimatum," don't listen to the radio when adults are talking about something called the Cuban missile crisis. Francesca had been only four at the time, her son's age now, when she and Zackary took him to the dinosaur park. A child of four, Francesca had understood something awful was happening.

"Are we all going to die?"

Yes, my sweet, we are all going to die — eventually. Inevitably. But let's hide it in rhymes.

> Now I lay me down to sleep,
> I pray the Lord my soul to keep.
> If I should die before I wake,
> I pray the Lord my soul to take.

Such a prayer—to make a child who really listens too terrified to sleep.

❧

How did the fight start? Zachary said the kid was a bully. The kid had pushed their son off the seesaw. A single child, Marco had a way of standing in place and inviting other kids into his orbit to play. Last she had seen was Marco sitting on one end of the seesaw, the other end empty in the air, waiting.

Marco wasn't crying. Marco never cried when he got hurt, as if everything was always his own fault—even in this instance, as his father stood over the other kid, shouting down the playground bully. Marco just went silent.

"You can't talk to me like this," the kid said. "My father is a lawyer."

At that Zachary, who was about to be disbarred, have his license to practise law irrevocably revoked, lost it.

"I don't care who your father is. You're a bully—a big, nasty bully. You pushed my son off the seesaw."

A circle of protective mothers gathered nearby. Francesca saw one of them confront Zachary. "The only bully I see is right here," pointing her finger at Zachary's chest, while anther mother took to her cellular phone.

"Zachary." Francesca took him by the hand. Zachary permitted her to lead him away. Once in the car, he burst into tears in front of their son! Marco sat silent and miserable in the back seat of Zachary's vehicle. The German-made Audi would be taken away by one of Zachary's judgment creditors later that week, even before Zachary declared personal bankruptcy.

"Marco doesn't need you to come to his defence. That's what playgrounds are all about. Little cesspools where kids learn the rules of engagement, or diplomacy. Not his middle-aged dad taking on some kid with a sense of hereditary entitlement."

The composition of bullies never changes.

"You will speak to my attorneys," Marco had said, the first time he spoke up against the imposition of an unfair parental dictate. Marco was about three, at the time. It was a line he had garnered from watching *The Littlest Millionaire*.

"And who, exactly, do you think are your attorneys?" Francesca had said. Adding, after a pause: "Your parents." She and Zachary were both still lawyers at the time, Zachary's disbarment not even a dimmer-switch in his eye. She and Zachary had laughed shamelessly at their son who had squirmed in his booster chair, at the dining-room table, for having dared to call out his parents for precisely what they were: "You pompous old windbags."

At that, Francesca and Zachary had really laughed, co-conspirators that they were in this nasty business of parenting—filling up Marco's beautiful beginner's mind with their own misguided agendas.

She wouldn't discover where her son had learned such big words until months later. The knowledge came when she stayed home with Marco for a week, still in her pajamas, after three back-to-back trials, which she had won, but which had left her utterly depleted and made her question the value of the work she was doing. Until her senior partner, Jack, summoned her back to assist him with his really big and important case, inquiring where the hell had she been.

She had spent that week watching endless re-runs of Walt Disney's *The Jungle Book*, while the nanny cleaned and made dinner and wondered what was wrong with her boss, why Francesca would not get out of pajamas but kept hugging Marco on the couch, and then suddenly, surrounded by jungle, Mrs. Elephant confronts Mr. Elephant for parading about with that big trumpeting trunk of his. My trunk, my jungle. "You pompous, old windbag."

That bullying in the playground, a transference — transferred anger, she now understands. It comes from a place of fear.

He had walked into her Law Chambers wearing his formal uniform, with all the medals jingling — the sergeant husband of one of her clients, but she didn't know this immediately. The receptionist called Francesca to tell her there was a police officer waiting to see her. When Francesca came forward into the reception area, she saw him, dominating the arena, not sitting the way clients normally sit in reception, but standing — his legs spread, his hands on his hips, a small grin upon his tanned and swarthy face — a stunning man, by all counts.

"What's this all about, officer?" she asked. Seeing her, he pulled himself up to his full height — towering a foot-and-a-half above her diminutive self. Clients were always surprised when she stood up from behind her desk or stood away from the podium in court. "Oh, you're much shorter than I thought."

"What do you think it's all about?" the officer said. "What have you done wrong?" With a smirk that made her prickle.

But like every honest, law-abiding person, the question caused her self-doubt. What had she done? Some failure to stop? That pigeon she had killed on Bond Street, speeding? Some case of mistaken identity? She felt herself blush. Involuntary confession of guilt.

He watched her squirm for a bit, and then told her his name. The proverbial penny dropped. Now Francesca realized he was the husband of Danielle L'Hereux, a woman she was representing, also a police officer, though lower in rank. Danielle had told Francesca her husband was abusive, but she loved him and still found him attractive, irresistible on occasion, especially in uniform. He would sometimes show up at her front door, late at night, and they would make love on the roof, with the children asleep in their beds. Once, he had threatened to throw Danielle off the roof. It was complicated. Danielle wouldn't report him for fear of the financial and other implications for their sons. But she had wanted Francesca to document this in her file in case anything like that ever did happen to Danielle.

Francesca was always amazed at the disconnection between the husbands her female clients described and the reality when she met them in person. She was bound by her clients' instructions and by what they told her to do or not do, but she wasn't bound to keep her mouth shut in the face of what this officer had just done—his abuse of office for self-serving and improper purposes. If he was off duty, he shouldn't be showing up in uniform. If he was on-duty, her office premises were not part of his patrol or parade ground, nor the dress uniform at all appropriate. He had crossed the line in showing up like this to confront Francesca directly when she knew him to be represented by his own counsel. Everything was wrong about this.

Whoosh of anger behind her eyes.

"You think you're going to intimidate me off your wife's case? You think the uniform is going to work like that, on me? This is an abuse of your office, officer." She looked into his flat, tanned face, saw the eyes widen. "Did you ever hear of the Magna Carta, officer? Do you think you're above the law? If you ever try a stunt like this again, I'll report you for trespass. Consider yourself warned. Now turn around and leave."

Astonishingly, he did. Like a little boy with his tail between his legs.

When she was certain he was out the door and out of earshot, she dropped her voice to a

stage whisper, remarking to the young receptionist, her only witness: "Pompous old windbag."
They both laughed.

Francesca twirled around and went back to
her work with renewed energy.

Open, Sesame*

*Or "Samsam," The grain = Sesamum
Orientale: hence the French, Sesame, ouvre-toi!*
—From *Ali Baba and the Forty Thieves,*
   Arabian Nights, translation by
   Sir Richard Burton

"Sherma, make a chicken broth overnight that we may drink of it upon our return home."

"Ms. Malotti, are you all right?"

Only then did Francesca realize she was dream-speaking about the chicken soup. Her Grenadian nanny's phone call had caught her in that deep stage of rapid eye movement, as if underwater and too slow to surface to realize they were in Grenada, her boy lay sound asleep in the bed beside her, naked and pink from the afternoon's play at shuffleboard with the kindly elderly couple who had watched him while his Momma slept poolside, the Gravol from the plane ride having finally taken effect; that she was who she was, where she was, that there were no meal plans to be made, no trial returnable Tuesday, no husband, no worries; she was on holiday, courtesy of the very wealthy and influential client, Issa Nefrutta, whose island hotel would shelter them for the week and who had assured her he would always be her friend.

"Your result is a perfect example of brilliant lawyer-skills and bad justice," Francesca's senior partner, Jack, had announced, when she told him she had obtained a stay of the Nefrutta Canadian divorce proceeding. Now the client's wife would have to litigate him in that "nest of thieves," according to the senior partner — Trinidad and Tobago — where the bulk of his assets, influence, and substantial connections lay. When the satisfied client, Issa Nefrutta, offered his successful counsellor this vacation, she'd had her choice of Barbados, Trinidad, or Grenada.

Francesca had vacationed in Barbados with her husband on their last trip together, a holiday made miserable by the pink eye contracted on the airplane. Her eyes had sealed shut each night; they could be loosened only by the tea bags she used as salves — frightening the night security in the executive lounge until he became used to her night-gowned presence, sleepless and despairing from a wordless anxiety she could not then name.

Sherma had placed a cup of tea in front of her the day her husband moved out. Francesca had been sitting at her kitchen table, staring at the wall, her chin on her fists, when the cup of tea appeared wordlessly on the table before her.

"Hire me," Sherma had said during their job interview. "I promise you will never regret it." The only thing Francesca had known about Sherma was that her last employment had been to care for a dying woman. "You will never regret it." She was true to her word, taking care of Francesca's boy, and Francesca. Sherma was an unexpected gift: a caregiver who took true care of the one who paid her.

So, Grenada it would be — as much a gesture of gratitude to Sherma as to Francesca. The client would have no idea about that, only that Francesca travelled with her boy and her nanny. Sherma would stay with her family but would help her with the plane ride and the child, as Francesca's fear of flying went up in proportion to her level of commitment to life — ferocious since becoming a mother. The fear incapacitated her. The plan was for Francesca to ingest enough Gravol to sleep through the flight, while Sherma watched over Marco.

The Gravol, she took, but the events of that day had required too much attention.

There were the many suitcases with which Sherma had arrived at the airport, filled with Mr. Noodle or other Canadian wonders for the extended Grenadian community back home. The extra weight cost Francesca four hundred dollars—a burden she could ill afford at this early stage of her separation. But she could also not bear the look of disappointment on Sherma's face at the prospect of renting a locker for the overweight luggage, the unspeakable disappointment of the intended recipients of Sherma's gifts.

And then there was the question at Grenadian Customs, on arrival. "What is in the suitcases?" Innocent Canadian lawyer that she was, Francesca answered truthfully that she had no idea whatsoever what was in the suitcases, deferring to Sherma. Sherma inclined toward her and spoke quickly and quietly to her ear. "Say we are guests of Issa Nefrutta." So Francesca drew her diminutive presence up as regally and authoritatively as she could, and announced: "We are guests of Issa Nefrutta." And, Open Sesame, the charm worked and the doors of Ali Baba's nest of thieves blew open, and

there was Stroud, Issa Nefrutta's personal chauf-
feur and former Chief of Police of the island,
waiting to receive Francesca, Francesca's son, and
Francesca's Grenadian nanny—no questions asked.
Francesca and her entourage and motley baggage
loaded into the Rolls Royce of the tinted and
bulletproof glass, without Francesca having to so
much as lift a finger or speak another word.

Francesca looked at Sherma with a new ap-
preciation of her wit, or, at very least, intuition of
the ways of the island from which she had de-
parted and to which she now returned with her
new employer, Francesca, and asked no questions
of the *non sequitur*: What is in the suitcases? We
are guests of Issa Nefrutta.

"Bullshit baffles brains," a favourite saying of
her now-former husband. Another: "You can fool
some of the people some of the time, most of
them all of the time."

This "We are guests of Issa Nefrutta" was the
only time Francesca had ever resorted to ruse.
Her only consolation was that, at the time, it was
the truth.

What was in Sherma's baggage?
Her brother had dropped something off at the

hotel where Francesca was staying as the guest of Issa Nefrutta. The brother had thought Sherma would be there, but she was with her Jehovah's Witnesses on that day. An insight, unrequested but delivered: Sherma had suffered heartbreak just before her departure for Canada. This was the reason for Canada. It was a very serious heartbreak. The man still lived in Grenada.

Francesca wondered: Was there a child?

This didn't strike her as the Sherma she knew, but then, she didn't know Sherma, she didn't know about the heartbreak. She didn't know Sherma at all. But she knew that Sherma was no empty vessel, not the sort that makes the most noise, or hides robbers. Her secrets lay within, would not be heaved into her mouth. She was a good and honest servant, true to her word.

Issa Nefrutta was not amused to learn that his Canadian lawyer had taken a public bus to the public marketplace. Francesca and Marco had boarded the bus with Sherma, who had flagged it down for them from the public streets. They were the only whites on the bus, and while on the bus her son inquired: "Momma, are we rich?" "Hush. No, sweetie." "I just saw a car like our one ..." There was no hushing him. He had no apprehension of harm. He was there with his Momma and Sherma, after all.

At the marketplace, with Sherma, they were safe. She bought them a coconut drink in a half shell of real coconut, and they milled about with Sherma's people, in Sherma's setting—safe, buying spices, beaded trinkets, a silk scarf at an Indian retailer, for home, being cared for by someone indigenous, of the island, who happened to live with them back in Canada.

The next day, Issa Nefrutta, who had heard of their escapades, insisted Francesca return with Stroud, on a tour of Grenada of a different sort. Did Issa contemplate that his former Chief of Police would take them to his former headquarters and show them the spot where the insurgents had been gunned down—bullet holes in the wall? Bullet holes in a supposedly bloodless revolution? Stroud counselled Francesca not to ask political questions, nor to seek answers of her own. But what kind of message was this to deliver to a lawyer? What to make of Stroud's advocacy against asking questions, against seeking answers.

And then, in the public marketplace, seated with her son in the backseat of the bullet-proof vehicle with the winged decoration on the front hood, Francesca watched in helpless horror through the tinted glass as the dark man with dreadlocks approached, raised his arms in combat-like position, and clicked the imaginary gun of his hand balanced in the crook of his arm, his crazed eye cocked on the target of her son. There is such a thing as the wrong place at the wrong time. In Issa Nefrutta's bulletproof Rolls Royce, they were such things. They were targets. Francesca knew Issa had moved his own children off the island for their safety. The legal arguments Francesca had used to persuade the Canadian Court of their "substantial connection" to Grenada, notwithstanding the move to safer shores, now came back to haunt her. Francesca and Marco were caught on the screen, and the illusionist with his fingers in front of the lighted projection machine—fluttered dove into gun.

On the island is a church with a bell. Stroud took them there. Beside the church is a graveyard. Stroud told them how, during the revolution, it was reported that persons had jumped from these cliffs. The bell has a rope. The rope dangled, irresistibly. And in the end, Francesca had not been able to resist. Her young son was appalled

when his mother did this. The bell rang for fu-
nerals and for weddings. Stroud told them this.
But on this day, Francesca rang it for herself and
her son. For the fact they were there, alive, and it,
the bell, was there. For the I don't know why. Just
to hear it ring. What it might sound like. For the
joy of it. For the anarchic hell of it.

By the time they got back to the hotel, the
whole island had heard. Issa Nefrutta had heard.
Issa Nefrutta's lawyer had rung the bell. How to
govern this Canadian lawyer of his—who had
no sense of decorum.

"Do not let your son pat the dogs on the beach.
They are wild dogs and full of disease."

Francesca watched, as the bitch was mounted,
one after another by the pack. Francesca studied
the expression on the bitch's face. What was it?
Passive? Barely interested? Accepting, almost, of
the exchange? But what did the bitch get out of
this? Protection, possibly? Food offerings? It was
not obvious. "What are they doing, Momma?"
"Pay no mind, they are just playing. That's what
dogs do, they play."

"Do not treat your servant too well. Servants respect authority; not kindness."

The next day, they were going to walk the beach together. Sherma did not possess a bathing suit. Francesca gave her a black swim suit — one of the four she had packed. This was the one from Florence with the scalloped collar, a fringe of green sparkling thread tied behind, at the neck. And she lent her the Florentine scarf of multi colours, to be worn like a sarong. It would blow in the ocean wind like a small glistening sail. The finishing piece — her white hat, with black lace fringe, Francesca's fanny hat, worn with the right side turned up saucily and the bow behind — a magnificent, seductive hat, one that bespoke success and even wealth. With these decorations and her large dark glasses, Sherma looked like a black Jacqueline Kennedy Onassis. She looked gorgeous, in the way of a vindicated young woman who can wear anything. Francesca would never again wear that bathing suit or that scarf or hat, because these belonged to Sherma now and would be forever part of this day — Sherma's day, this was her day, and Francesca walked behind her, ten paces behind collecting sea shells, as Sherma strode, her long black legs making modest tracks in the sand, with Francesca's pink son at her side, and Francesca watching the sensation her servant created—the returning woman, could hear the word on the island, the word in town, the word that was out—that Sherma had returned, that Sherma had returned in style. The best vengeance, absolutely, is to live well. That day Sherma vibrated—an instrument in tune with her world.

And what was Francesca's part of this day? That she could aid and abet another woman.

"Ms. Malotti, you will never know what this has meant to me. I am so very grateful ..."

Francesca knew. No thanks were required. This was vindication by extension.

Do not treat your servant too well ...

"Do not walk the beach alone at night. If you wish privacy, my security guards will follow you, at a distance, from the shore."

The Ferryman

"Ferry me across the water,
Do, boat-man, do."
"If you've a penny in your purse,
I'll ferry you."

"I have a penny in my purse,
And my eyes are blue;
So ferry me across the water,
Do, boat-man, do."

"Step into my ferry boat,
Be they black or blue,
And for the penny in your purse
I'll ferry you."

Francesca's son had to memorize this song about the ferryman so he could sing it as one of the Toronto Children's Chorus by their return to Canada. Alone on the beach, of a morning, unaware of Issa's security guards or of Issa's eyes, Francesca sat cross-legged on the pink sand facing the ocean, her son tucked in the crib of her crossed legs, the Introductory Songbook of the Grade 1 level of the Royal Conservatory of Music open in front of them, singing with a passion for the boatman and the woman whose colour of eyes to the boatman was completely immaterial, who was doing it, if at all, for the penny in the purse, thinking about the ones who carry us across the water, who are rarely the ones who meet us on the other shore, wondering what these words of Christina G. Rossetti were doing in a Vocal Repertoire Album intended, supposedly, for children? And what of that *non sequitur*: "I have a penny in my purse and my eyes are blue." What currency is blue eyes? And whose boat had Francesca stepped into? What act of faith did this take, black or blue, whether penny in her purse, or otherwise — she, a woman, so far from home? A woman, alone. A woman with child. Alone.

"I will always be your friend."

She was supposed to meet him for cocktails. She assumed at the hotel bar, beside the pool, where she could keep watch over her son, unlike the day of their arrival.

What had the elderly couple that had cared for her little boy thought of this mother, while she, unconscious with the delayed affects of the Gravol, had slept? There is a picture of Francesca, asleep on a lounge chair, curled fetal, with a book of short stories by Alice Munro gripped in her right hand, pressed beneath her cheek, her face closed with sleep, but for the open mouth. Seeing this picture developed, which her son must have taken, Francesca imagines the sound of snores, possibly drool. Around the hat with the black lace fringe is a halo of fuchsia hibiscus her son carefully picked and arranged in preparation for this picture of his Momma.

Now the son protects his mother. There will be no cocktails with Issa and Francesca. It has turned cold. At 6:30 p.m., the sun sets, the wind is up from the ocean. Francesca assumes Issa has stood her up, while Issa, from his perch in the executive suite, has assumed likewise. Francesca, delivered from an unwanted encounter, is relieved. She takes her boy to their room and gives him a hot bath. She follows his hot bath with her own, and they both retire early.

Francesca sends Issa Nefrutta a final bill, upon her return to Canada, which reflects her sense of the true value of the result she has achieved on his behalf. She sends the bill, along with her gracious thanks for his gift of this holiday — the first she has taken in years. Francesca has weighed most carefully the issue of her bill. What recourse does she have if he refuses to pay? She senses what he has intended by this trip. It becomes very awkward to invoice him, having received this holiday as his gift. But ultimately, not difficult at all. The bill reflects what her services are worth, what she herself is worth. She hasn't asked for the gift. Nor has she abused his hospitality, nor deceived him in any way. She simply does not deliver his latest expectation, which is outside their retainer, in any event. What harm in that? She has remained his true and loyal servant, will not compromise the solicitor and client relationship. For the penny in your purse, not for anything else, has she carried him across the water. So, Francesca holds her peace during the silence that has followed on her bill. As the morning begins to dawn on a month following her return, Scheherazade suspends her story to the next time and extends her life thereby, just as surely as Francesca rang a church bell, once upon a time, in Grenada.

Sins of the Father

Francesca opens her eyes to the grey light of winter dawn, the tail of her son's golden retriever, Isis, thumping the mattress, the pant of its stinky breath in her own stale mouth. Over the dog's head, she sees a photograph on the bedside table.

The photograph is of her former husband, Zachary, and his latest woman, taken in some southern destination, wearing diving gear and standing beside oxygen tanks. "It's the fastest way to disappear into another world, another life," Zachary told her once, when she had worried about his risk-taking holidays with their only son, Marco, diving with sharks. Not surprising Zachary would want to escape into another world, pursued as he always is by his creditors. Only days ago, she'd received a phone message on her voice mail. Still, and after over 20 years of separation, the voice on the message demanded immediate response from Zachary Hamilton or this matter would go "into collection."

Slowly, Francesca retrieves the night before —she and Marco had arrived at his father's cottage after dark, watched the snow fall over a frozen lake from the screened-in porch, brought in the luggage, stomped the snow off their boots; watched the movie *Jeremy Buttons* over a bottle of scotch and ate a late-night bowl of noodles Marco made. She had cried her eyes out at the story of Jeremy Buttons, a man who lives his life backwards, born an old man to die a baby. She does not remember much after that.

It dawns on her that her adult son, Marco, must have put her to bed in the master bedroom.

Still pasted to the bed, mouth drooling onto the pillow, Francesca doesn't immediately get up, right hand patting the dog's head. She lies there, listening to its thumping tail, its throaty golden retriever joy in the morning, and contemplates the ironies: best sleep of her life in her former husband's bed! Who would have imagined?

"Did you ask your father's permission?" Francesca asked Marco, on the drive north.

"Of course, I did. Dad said it was his gift to us both, for Papa Giovanni. He said to tell you he's sorry for your loss."

"That was good of him," Francesca said.

Gift, she thought. *Doesn't that mean something given without condition, without strings attached?* She disliked herself for scepticism, mourning her loss of trust along with so much else.

Something is upsetting her. Some further residue from last night.

The painting! She saw it hanging above the couch. Her late father's painting. Her son had taken it from her basement. She'd seen him down there some weeks ago, flipping through the racks. She thought he was mourning in his own way, and let him be. Now she understands. Zachary would never give anything but that he expected in return. She remembers Zachary saying to her at the funeral home, as the video of her father's paintings rotated in carousel on the screen: "If you have any extra paintings laying around, I wouldn't mind one or two, for the cottage." *Over my dead body*, Francesca had thought, but said nothing, not wanting to make a scene, for Marco's sake. Marco's taking and giving of the painting was in consideration for this time together, she now realizes. But Marco didn't ask his mother's permission as he had of his father.

More than the fact of her late father's painting hanging on her former husband's walls is the fact of the taking and not asking. The painting wasn't Marco's to give.

The dog Isis, not having had as much scotch the night before, is thumping its tail now vigorously against the mattress. At the opening of the human's eyes, its throaty moan rises to a howl. So, Francesca gets up and lets Isis out the porch door, where it promptly does its rolls, before yellowing the snow. Isis looks back at her, snout full of snow and expectant golden retriever smile, as if to say: "Won't you come out to play?" So quickly, Francesca dresses in snow pants and coat, pulls on her boots, and takes a walk with Isis to the frozen lake. Most of the cottages and trailers are closed up for the winter. The odd truck or vehicle in a shovelled driveway signifies some human presence. She smells brewing coffee.

When she returns with Isis, her son has not yet stirred. So she makes herself an instant coffee and sits in the screened-in porch with the dog at her feet, still dressed in her snow pants and coat.

That's when she notices the *KAMA SUTRA* sitting on an end table, exposed to the elements, its beautiful emerald and gold dustcover slightly puckered from the damp. It must have been left there recently, not to have experienced more damage. Barnes & Noble Booksellers, only $24.98 says the sticker. Inside the flap:

> The *Kama Sutra* is a two-thousand-year-old mystical treatise on sexuality. This beautiful edition pairs the ancient text with richly detailed illustrations from the renowned archives of the University of Cambridge. Chaturvedi Badrinath's introduction places Vatsyayana's text in its philosophical context, explaining the Eastern belief in the unity of the physical and spiritual and its role in the understanding of sexual pleasure. The classical text, coupled with the brilliant artwork, combine to create a magical book every reader will enjoy and treasure.

"Coupled." Fitting choice of words, she thinks. Flipping through the pictures, Francesca feels herself blush. She and Marco's father never did it that way. And what of this pose? How can the human body twist itself up into such a pretzel?

She must have it. If her former husband can take her late father's painting, she can take the book. Zachary likely won't even connect the dots or notice it missing, and if he does, won't dare ask for it back. Besides, with so little respect for the book to leave it exposed to the elements, a book to be "enjoyed and treasured," Zachary doesn't deserve it, just as he hadn't deserved her.

Lying

Grampa Hamilton, Zachary's father, told stories differently than Papa Giovanni, Francesca's father. Observant from a very young age, Marco noticed this. Grampa Hamilton's stories changed every time he told them. By his last telling of this story, there with fifty German airplanes, not five, and Grandpa Hamilton outsmarted them all. And the nurses that greeted Grandpa Hamilton back in England upon his return flight sat six to his lap, not one or two.

When Papa Giovanni told a story, it was the same every time. Like the story he told about taking his nephews camping, and how they had hung the fish they caught off the back of Papa's truck, and how the nephews had all peed on it every morning. The eldest nephew, (later a businessman who marketed the shares of his gold mine on the Toronto stock exchange, in which venture Papa Giovanni lost a lot of money) sold the fish to some American tourist for 20 bucks. How upset Papa Giovanni was about the misrepresentation! To the last day Papa Giovanni told this story, he warned Marco never to invest in equities, especially if you're related to the owner of the supposed gold mine. But the thing, the thing about Papa's stories was the consistency. The fish didn't become a moose, as it would have in Grandpa Hamilton's stories and the nephews didn't all become billionaires in some prosperous Alberta pipeline. Papa Giovanni was upset with each re-telling about the misrepresentation of the fish, but it was the same upset, not more or less agitated. Selling a stinky fish that all the nephews had peed upon for 20 bucks wasn't right at any price.

The lying starts young. Francesca knew Marco had taken a $20 bill from her wallet because of the post-it note she found on the floor. It was her habit to affix reminder notes to the bills in her wallets, a memory aid in a place to which she went every day. When Marco hastily removed the $20, he must not have noticed the post-it note fall to the floor. At first, Marco denied taking it.

"I'm hungry after school. I wanted a hamburger, and you don't like it when I use my debit card because of the extra charges."

That much was true. Francesca was trying to

teach the then-teenaged Marco fiscal responsibility. Making a debit for a hamburger which carried bank charges almost equal to the hamburger made no fiscal sense.

"So, let's review all the possible choices, Marco. For one, you could have come to me and told me you need a bigger allowance. You could have told me why. You might have considered an after-school job, flipping those burgers yourself a couple of evenings a week. But of all the choices you could have made, you picked the worst. You stole from your mother."

At that, Francesca burst into tears.

"Your father stole from me," she said between sobs.

Her words registered shock. Then silence. It was the first time she had ever given Marco a clue to the origins of the separation, which occurred when Marco was only six. Then Marco broke into tears. Together, they sat on the stairs in the foyer of the home she had managed to salvage from Zachary's creditors, arms around each other, and both wept. It was the first time Francesca heard her son cry since his voice had changed. She knew from his tears that all would be well. Marco had a sense of right from wrong. Maybe love enough for his mother not to want to hurt her, not to push the envelope too far. He was becoming a real man.

The next time she would hear sobs from her son would be at his Papa Giovanni's funeral. And all the real men who heard those sobs had started sobbing, too.

Irrevocably Revoked

One of the secretaries in the Law Chambers brought her a copy of the *Ontario Reports*, page open to where Zachary's disbarment was announced.

"Is this your former husband?" the secretary asked.

Francesca read the page, felt the heat rise to her cheeks.

The shame was for her choice. Her choice of a man she hadn't really known at the time she married him.

"I'm sorry," the secretary said, "Jack thought you should know. He said he didn't want you to be sabotaged by what you didn't know." Seeing Francesca colour, the secretary said: "It's a sign of his respect for you." It was the secretary's maternal instinct to protect not only Jack, but also

Jack's relations, the smooth sailing of Jack's firm. Francesca had learned almost everything about life and law from Jack, and was still learning.

"What else did Jack say?"

"He said 'poor kid.'"

With Zachary's first stint of trouble with the Law Society, Jack had defended him, for the sake of Francesca, his then junior lawyer. Zachary got off lightly, that time, with only a suspension of two months. But Zachary had repeated the same mistake. He next fraudulently misrepresented his client's resources. On the faith of Zachary's misrepresentation, five financial institutions advanced funds to Zachary's client, later lost when the client disappeared. There seemed to be no rhyme or reason for why Zachary went out onto such a limb for a client — tarnishing his own reputation in the process.

"'Poor kid, with that name,' Jack said. 'It's a good thing your son doesn't become a lawyer. He would never escape the name.'"

The summer of his father's disbarment, Marco had a student job at a pool. It was the last summer before engineering, and he went to work every day with the biography of Einstein — more to impress the girls, who purchased tickets for their entry fee and their locker. Francesca didn't want Marco to be sabotaged by what he didn't know. She asked him to have a seat. "Let's talk."

Surprisingly, Marco volunteered what had happened at the pool that very day. Someone had gotten into a girl's locker through fraudulent means. This person had gone up to one of the female summer-student staff in the locker room and said she'd forgotten her combination and begged the staff person to let her into the locker. The fraudster had described everything that was in the locker, so that when the gullible staff person opened the door, everything was exactly as described, and the fraudster made off with the stolen garments and contents. Every city staff person working the pool that day had been made to swear an affidavit as to what they knew or didn't know, and as to the trustworthiness of the person who had innocently opened the locker door. Otherwise, the city management would have fired her.

Sometimes there are gifts in life, these cracks in the shells of things that admit light.

"You see what damage that liar has done? It's not just the girl who lost her clothes, it's the person who almost got fired, and it's the closing of the pool during the investigation in the middle of a Toronto heatwave, and it's all of you summer students who had to take the time out of your productive day to write out what you knew and didn't know. So much collateral damage ..." And then: "Marco, has your dad told you what is happening with him, these days?"

"He said he didn't steal any trust funds." That much Francesca knew from the page in the *Ontario Reports* was at least true, but Zachary was always one to minimize the gravity of his choices.

"I don't know everything yet. Your dad and I are going to speak later this week. I want you to know, that if you ever need to talk to someone about this, I will help you find the right person. It doesn't have to be me. It doesn't have to be your dad. It can be someone completely neutral, who will keep what you discuss in absolute confidence."

"Why should I need to speak about it? I didn't do anything wrong."

"Put it this way, Marco, you still have the gift of your unmade choices. When I was growing up, I was always so very proud of your Papa Giovanni."

At that, it was as if the proverbial penny dropped. Marco's eyes welled up with tears.

She must have it. And have it, she does. Without a second thought. Reparations. At very least, she has the book. And every time she looks at it, displayed on the delicate Victorian luggage rack with the embroidered straps, sitting at the end of the chaise lounge in her master bedroom, this eye-for-an-eye theft of the *KAMA SUTRA* gives Francesca an instant pleasure, more than even the pictures in the book. In fact, she has never read the whole book. It sits there, like a possibility. Perhaps she will finally take the time to read it, in her old age, and contemplate all the ways she might have done it. With what kind of man. Had she been reckless and abandoned, like her risk-taker husband, Zackary ... No, rather, had she been coupled with a real man, one who would have treasured her, one who could tell his tales in a constant and consistent manner, in the unity of a physical and holy expression of love. What wondrous and mystical variations-on-a-theme they might have made, what a joyous instrument she might have been and how lovingly she would have practised.

Newton's Third Law

Mrs. Iryna Buriak receives her mother's inheritance and uses it not to pay down the mortgage that collaterally secures Mr. Buriak's monument business, but to secretly retain a divorce lawyer.

Thirty-five years ago, at the age of 20, she had started in the monument business as a receptionist working for Mr. Buriak, Senior. Iryna had been beautiful, then — fulsome, blonde, her face as yet untouched by cigarettes, alcohol, or Mr. Bohdan Buriak, Junior. She continued on as a receptionist after marriage at the age of 22 to the boss's son through two children and 33 years.

Because of Mrs. Iryna Buriak's stubborn refusal to use her inheritance from her late mother to pay down his business mortgage, Mr. Bohdan Buriak sends his wife into the cold storage room where the monuments are kept, to take inventory. Cold storage is where Mr. Bohdan Buriak always sends Mrs. Iryna Buriak to punish her.

Cold storage after she bought a Christmas table-cloth. Cold storage after she purchased winter boots for their youngest son — Yurij had out-grown his boots before the boxing-day sales before Ukrainian Christmas and Iryna Buriak didn't think the child should struggle through snow in boots two sizes too small. Cold storage for not buying day-old bread ...

After two weeks of taking inventory of the marble headstones and plaques, now 55 years of age, Mrs. Iryna Buriak contracts bronchitis, but recovers quickly.

Mrs. Iryna Buriak goes to the Buduchnist Credit Union and withdraws her inheritance.

Mrs. Iryna Buriak's lawyer sends a letter announcing her client's desire to separate "as amic-ably and as respectfully as possible." Upon receiving it, Mr. Bohdan Buriak has his book-keeper send his wife a letter terminating her employment. Her termination is for "unspecified cause." He does not pay the minimum severance required by the Employment Standards Act.

She takes her first day off work in 35 years, not counting the days following the birth of each of their two sons, Danylo Buriak, now 19 and Yurij Buriak, now 11. The youngest, Yurij, was a surprise, born to Mrs. Iryna Buriak in her 44th year.

On her first day off work, Mrs. Iryna Buriak removes Mr. Bohdan Buriak's coin collection from the lower drawers of the armoire in the matrimonial bedroom. She drives north to visit a loyal cousin, Michael Morozenko. Together, they photograph each of the coins. She leaves the coins in Michael Morozenko's cellar, for safe keeping. The photos are sent to a coin specialist, for valuation. She tells the specialist to be on particular lookout for a Ukrainian coin that first landed on Canadian soil in the heel of Mr. Buriak, Senior's boot.

Mrs. Iryna Buriak's lawyer writes a second letter, advising the coins have been removed to safe keeping and for valuation, while urging Mr. Bohdan Buriak to retain counsel and to re-instate his wife's salary.

Mr. Bohdan Buriak refuses to hire counsel. He refuses to re-instate his wife's salary.

Mr. Bohdan Buriak threatens the wife's counsel with criminal charges for harbouring "stolen goods." He is certain his wife's lawyer has his coins.

Mrs. Iryna Buriak commences an Application for Divorce.

Their first time in court, Mrs. Iryna Buriak passes the hours waiting for the case to be called by doing her needlepoint. Patiently, she stitches beautifully coloured letters onto a pillow, as if she were brushing colours onto a Ukrainian Easter egg, each stitch a needle into a Voodoo doll: "Don't Dare Sleep." She will leave the pillow on Mr. Bohdan Buriak's side of the bed.

Mr. Bohdan Buriak refuses to leave the matrimonial home. He will not co-operate in a joint listing of the property. A motion will have to be brought for its sale.

Mr. Bohdan Buriak will insist upon his own real estate agent.

He will take down the signs of her real estate agent, hide these behind the enormous obstructing trunk of the grand maple tree in the back yard.

Mrs. Iryna Buriak goes grocery shopping. In a frenzy of hammering, measuring, sawing, he constructs drywall down the centre of the home. She returns home with bags of groceries, only to find upon opening the front door, that she must turn this way or that to enter from the right or the left half of the front entrance. Upstairs, she sees her husband has mounted the drywall up and over the matrimonial bed, such that it is impossible for either to get a proper sleep or to change the sheets.

Yet another motion is brought, to compel Mr. Bohdan Buriak to remove the drywall and to vacate the home, pending its sale. He is ordered to pay Mrs. Iryna Buriak's costs.

Mr. Bohdan Buriak goes to live with his elderly father, and from his new perch in the Buriak paternal home, Mr. Bohdan Buriak continues to harass, to the point of terror, Mrs. Iryna Buriak.

The next motion is for Court approval to a bona fide third-party purchase offer to the house, for which Mr. Bohdan Buriak is unreasonably withholding his consent. At the eleventh hour, he relents and permits the offer.

The purchase price drops, after Mr. Bohdan Buriak contacts the prospective purchaser and warns of mould in the bathroom off the master bedroom.

Another motion is brought, to make the diminution of sale price between the first and second offer come out of Mr. Bohdan Buriak's notional half proceeds of sale and to find Mr. Bohdan Buriak in contempt of court. The contempt motion is denied, for now, with a hefty admonishment. Mr. Bohdan Buriak is again ordered to pay the wife's costs.

"The Karma bus just left and he's not on it," Mrs. Iryna Buriak says to her lawyer, as she watches Mr. Bohdan Buriak leave the courtroom, that day. "I almost feel sorry for him. No, I don't feel sorry for him. Maybe someday I will."

Action and Reaction

I, Iryna Buriak, make oath and say as follows ...
To hell with the affidavit format. Been there.
Done that. I'm taking control of my own story.
When you see the "I" it is me, Iryna, doing the
telling. Doesn't matter to whom. Just assume it's
to you. Just know it's the truth. This is my story:

I went to see a lawyer first. Then, my lawyer sent
me off to do some homework. Tax bill, utility
bills, trying to figure out expenses toward property division. When I started looking for the
paperwork, I realized it was all gone. Bohdan is an
anal record keeper, and everything was gone. I
think he has a plan. He hasn't actually gone to a
lawyer, yet. But he is preparing to do something.

The day he got the letter of intent to separate
was the day I removed the coins.

Bohdan sent me into cold storage.

I got pneumonia.

He fired me.

He got served that afternoon.

My lawyer got an emergency hearing, on a
cancellation, three days later. His lawyer couldn't
figure out how we got to court so fast. Served on
a Monday and we were in court on Thursday.

Bohdan wanted to change the date of separation to say we'd separated 10 years earlier, so my claim to an equal share of everything would be out of time. You'd think his lawyer would have said something about how stupid that made him look, with Yurij age 11, but no, he had to hear it from the judge.

The judge requested a meeting with the two lawyers in chambers. My lawyer told me over lunch what the judge had said. We were sitting in a Chinese restaurant, after court, and I was cackling hard at how the judge had summed up Bohdan—"Another Ukrainian guy with a God complex."

I wonder if the judge knew the history—Ukraine, the victim nation—bullied by Russia, Germany, Poland. There is something to be said for the inflated ego of survivors. My cousin Michael Morozenko thinks we're a pack of losers, always on the losing side of history.

The judge told both lawyers he'd had one of these Ukrainian guys in his first year of practice —a husband who'd had a bunch of his drunk Bohunk buddies over to the home while his wife was out, and damned if they didn't put up drywall right down the centre of the house. "It must be a Ukrainian thing," he said, because he'd never thought he'd live to see that one again.

The Squeaky Floor

My late mother had a twisted, wicked sense of humour. I must have inherited it. Never malicious. When Bohdan moved to the basement, in the period before the judge ordered him out, Bohdan built himself this lovely room that was completely finished. He'd go there to sleep. He is a very light sleeper. So, at night, I would set my alarm for two o'clock in the morning to go outside and have a cigarette. I would creep back into the house. There was one spot in the hall. The floor creaked horribly.

I would stand in the hallway, exactly where the creaks were, and go squeaky squeaky, until I saw the light go on downstairs. I'd creep back into my room and go back to sleep, and he'd be up all night. Something my late mother would do. I swear, she must have been whispering in my ears. Squeak the floors.

I don't think he ever figured it out.

Wake him up, wake him up, wake him up.

That was my big retaliation. Didn't cost me anything. Didn't hurt anybody ...

Two years, every night. Squeaky, squeaky, squeaky, wake him up, wake him up, wake him up.

And I was always able to go back to sleep, completely refreshed in the morning, dreams of the peace that comes from further vengeance dancing in my head.

I think that's when Bohdan went to the doctor and got sedatives.

Random Acts of Harmless Revenge

Before I gave him back all the keys to the company car, I would, every now and then, randomly set off the car alarms.

Bohdan would be getting his key into the front door, and off the cars would go, and he'd have to run down the drive to figure out what was going on.

After I bought my new car, from the costs the judge ordered against Mr. Buriak, I left the old car keys on the kitchen table.

My Mother's Contents

Momma had died the year before I started the divorce proceedings and I had boxes of her stuff stored in the basement. Her stuff had been there for a couple of years. That's when, all of a sudden, things started to disappear from the home. I wasn't really aware of it. I happened to go down to do laundry and as I was turning, I saw, what's missing? I started to go through the boxes. All the framed photos of me and my kids — all gone. Now I have no pictures of me with Danylo and Yurij. I was usually the one taking photos at family events. I was rarely in a picture with the kids. Now I have no pictures, at all.

It was like he wanted my actual life to have never existed. Gone. Disposed of.

I had a sentimental attachment to some of my Momma's stuff that I took with me, after she died, and stored it in the basement. There was a little antique dresser, with a swivel mirror, that was my grandmother's — poof, gone. I began doing the laundry again. There was this box on the work-bench. I labelled all my boxes when I was moving. I turned around and it was labelled with the contents he had put in there — "old iron" Where's my iron — what old iron? I removed the tape carefully and it was this old cast-iron press that they had put hot coals into back in the Ukraine — they were my Baba's irons. And my Baba's old hand sickle brought from Ukraine. I took the sickle out of the box. There were all these jars of screws and nuts and bolts. Kind of weighed it. Replaced Baba's irons and sickle with jars of screws. Re-taped the whole box and left it alone.

I started to go through the house. One day

while he was at work, I lifted all the artwork off the walls, put it all in my car and drove it to my girlfriend's. It was stuff we had collected together, stuff that had really spoken to me when we'd bought it and hung it. He doesn't care about art, only its monetary value.

Appendix: The Useless Organ That Kills

"Momma, I don't feel good." It was just after Ukrainian Christmas. "Ah, you just ate too much crap. Did you go to the bathroom? Well, go to sleep. If you need me, come into the bedroom, you know where I am."

About two o'clock in the morning, I heard Yurij in the bathroom, throwing up. Yurij was about 12 or 13 years old, at the time.

I rinsed Yurij's mouth. I washed Yurij's face. "Do you think you can lie down?"

"Momma, can I come in and lie down with you?" I thought, something is really wrong. He was hot. At one point, "I feel better now, I'm going to go back to bed."

When I woke him up in the morning, he was on fire. He rolled over and moaned at me. "My stomach."

"Lie down on your back, show me where.

Lower right quadrant. Get dressed, I'm going to take you down to urgent care."

Doctor examined him, hit the spot, kid jack-knifed. Had ultrasound. I ran outside to phone his father to let him know what's happening.

"Chances are he has appendicitis."

"I could have told you that, last night."

So, the kid suffered all night, because his father wouldn't communicate with me, not even for the sake of his own kid.

Once we got into the room, I gave his father a call and gave him the room number. He asked to speak to Yurij. Yurij was going to be taken for surgery within the next half hour.

"So, is your Dad coming?"

"No, he's not coming. He told me he's not coming because you're here."

I don't get the games people play through the kids, to make each other miserable. But this was different. This was Mr. Bohdan Buriak not even wanting to see his youngest son, before surgery.

Acorns don't fall too far from the tree

Yurij's grandfather, Mr. Buriak, Senior, called me out of the blue.

"Is Yurij home?"

"No, he's out with friends."

"Well, I'd like to see him."

"Well, you'll have to speak to him. It's not up to me anymore."

"I'm going to come by your place."

"No, you're not. I'd prefer you didn't."

"It's not nice, Yurij doesn't return my calls. His own grandfather."

"Well, really, it's up to Yurij. All I can do is relay the message and encourage him."

"I'd like to stop by."

"As I said before, I'd prefer that you didn't."

"Yurij should be able to say who he sees."

"No doubt. However, any visit won't be here."

"I haven't talked to my grandson in a long time. We don't know if you're keeping him from us."

"Hold it right there. First of all, the boy is almost 18 years old. I don't have much control over who he sees or doesn't. He's able to make his own choices. At this point, he chooses not to see you. I can't change his mind. And I'm not prepared to try to change his mind. It comes full circle."

"I don't know what happened to your marriage with Bohdan."

"Interesting, because when I took steps to try to talk to you, you took a different approach. You surgically removed me from the family."

"Bohdan and I, we don't talk anymore."

"That's too bad, because you're father and son."

"I don't know what happened. Bohdan doesn't talk to us."

"Again, not my problem."

Then, I took pity on the old man. I could see his big, red, perplexed face.

"Did you ever try listening?"

Dead silence.

"Well, I'd still like to talk to Yurij."

Newton's Law for Ukrainians

For every action there is an equal and opposite reaction, except in the case of the Ukrainian male. The action is like running into a monumental stone—absolutely immovable.

The Coin Return

The closing ceremony reflects the opening, which was the taking of the coins.

Our lawyers are in place. Except Mr. Bohdan Buriak's lawyer has, inexplicably, sent one of his young law clerks. Bohdan doesn't seem to care. He is too busy hating my lawyer.

So, it starts. This is the deal. What the lawyers

have worked out. I have to give back all the coins and he is going to verify that each and every one is there. Out comes a coin. The coin is located on page 36 of the list. Bohdan turns each coin upside down, backwards and forward, and slowly acknowledges receipt.

Out comes the next coin. Same process.

There are coins he comments upon — like the coin from 1978 — that was a "very bad year. A disaster of a year." The young clerk asks: "Oh, Mr. Buriak, what made that a bad year?"

My lawyer answers: "It was the year they got married. You weren't even born yet."

Day One, we've completed one of the five boxes needing acknowledgment.

We adjourn. I have to re-organize the boxes, in accordance with the lists, to make the coin exchange go faster. It takes about 17 hours for me to do that. We come back, the next week.

As each page is completed, Mr. Bohdan Buriak signs, witnesses sign. Toward the end of the second day, he begins to deflate. It is almost as if the anger is going out of the balloon. This was the last thing he has to hold onto, his anger over the coins. He begins to understand that the marriage is at an end. He finally realizes that, once these coins are done, it is done. We are done. This will be the last time we sit in the same room together. I am not going to search him out. He is never going to search me out. There is never going to be any hide and seek, seek and find. We have no reason to see each other, ever again. No action. No reaction. We are done. Stopped. Ended. Too tired even to feel sad.

The Ultimate Revenge

I forgive him. Something Bohdan will never do.

I feel really sorry for him. He's going to end up a miserable old man.

Oh well, that's his funeral.

Because he doesn't have any outside interests. All Bohdan can do is sit and stew. I'm too bloody busy. I have my Ukrainian dancing. My needle point. My Ukrainian singing. My Ukrainian women's organization, which is like a sisterhood.

I forgive him. He will never reciprocate.

He would first have to forgive himself, as I have forgiven myself. Have come to be at peace with myself. And so:

Peace be with you, Bohdan.

Dead silence.

Peace be with you, Bohdan.

Dead silence.

Peace be with you, Bohdan.

A monument to cold storage silence.

Toilet Bowl Blues

Joshua and Marcia were tumultuous lovers. Their arguments exploded from the windows of Joshua's glass factory, open even in winter and late into the night. Joshua Bevis had a decorative glass business and owned the building next to my father's sign shop on Dufferin Avenue. Our family lived in the apartment above the sign shop. Joshua's glass factory was on the second floor of his building. He rented out the main floor. As a girl growing up, I would watch Joshua through the window of our family bathroom. Joshua worked mostly nights with Marcia, his platinum blonde girlfriend. Joshua and Marcia used ovens to affix the decorations to the surfaces of the glass. These were the days, pre-air-conditioning. Joshua's second floor must have been sweltering. I only ever remember Joshua wearing an under-shirt, even in winter, the black hairs sprouting from his armpits and around his neck. Joshua and Marcia never married. They had a lifelong, on-again-off-again relationship, dating back to the swing, wartime years, well before my birth.

Marcia painted the artwork on the glasses. She seemed to me the soul of patience, bent quietly over her artwork, even as Joshua's bellowed commands could be heard alongside the odd shatter of glass. Every Christmas our father would be gifted a set of glasses that stayed downstairs in the sign-shop office, behind the long desk, where my father kept alcohol for customers and other male secrets his daughters were never supposed to see. One set of glasses had the twelve signs of the zodiac, with men and women dancing in unusual poses. I had to unwrap each glass carefully, so it would fit back into the box of twelve, undetected. If Marcia could paint them, why could my father's daughters not look?

In my early teen years, my parents would leave their daughters at home in the apartment so they could go out on Saturday night dates. After their dates they always slept late into Sunday morning. Lobster claws or petits fours and other leftover wonders would greet us in the refrigerator from restaurants with names like The Ports of Call or George's Spaghetti House. Their date nights added new colourful swizzle sticks to the cocktail collection, with palm trees and flags of different lands. We were on our own, Sunday mornings, until our parents emerged late from the bedroom. Monday mornings, Joshua would report to our father on the arguments my older sister, Elizabeth, and I had, our screaming so violent it had worried Joshua enough to almost call the police. "I thought they were going to kill each other."

There were nights I worried the same about Marcia and Joshua.

What set us off? Elizabeth would call me "fatso" but then bribe our little sister Rose with pizza, so Elizabeth got to watch whatever she wanted on our single TV. I had to stand there beside her at the sink while Elizabeth washed and I dried, waiting endlessly for her to finish a single plate. I could have read a chapter of *War and Peace* before she moved on to the next dish. Why couldn't she just pile them up and let me dry later? But no. She-who-made-the-rules-and-regulations insisted, so what could have been done in 10 minutes, took hours.

Our washing of dishes was nothing like that of our parents—Dad commandeering the tea towel, while Mom washed, his pecks to her neck, then that playful splash of soap suds, flick of the towel to her beautiful backside, and their dancing to CFRB on the radio, AM frequency. While Elizabeth vacated the kitchen in disgust, I was always comforted by their gentle affection toward each other, the way they found such joy in something as simple as doing dishes. After dishes, Dad went downstairs to the sign shop, to work again, while Mom focused on her ironing. Our job, as kids, was to study, to get an education that would free us from their labours. Nothing made my mother happier about me than when I brought home the "A's." She believed I had important work to do with my life.

The name calling, the "fatso" and "stupid" really triggered me. My obedience in the face of my older sister's abuse is what fascinates me now; it laid the foundation for what was to come—a high tolerance for pain. Our parents, who loved and revolved around each other, didn't seem to notice, or maybe thought this rivalry between siblings was normal. I don't remember seeing any manuals on parenting about the apartment, if such existed, at the time. Working as hard as they did on their nesting partnership, they didn't have much time to read.

Joshua was a drinker, which might explain why Marcia did all the fine brushwork.

Still, Joshua must have had his soft and sentimental side, because Joshua gave glasses to each of my sisters and me for our weddings, marked with the name of the bride and groom and date of our weddings — even when I got married twice. He and Marcia were never invited to any of these occasions.

Once, my mother invited Marcia to tea. Marcia wore her platinum hair long, never cut it to behave her age. (Mom was big on behaving.) Marcia was a working woman. My mother had all her babies in the 1950s, had a husband who supported her and a dream for her daughters that we would all go to a private girls' school, would one day become "Ladies of Loretto." She got to see at least that dream fulfilled.

Joshua knew I had become a lawyer. So, when he encountered landlord and tenant problems with the downstairs commercial tenant, Joshua changed the locks and came to see me. I was in my first year of practice. Joshua's tenant had moved out over the previous weekend, taking almost everything — including the toilet bowl — but leaving behind a piece of heavy equipment. While the toilet bowl was clearly a fixture and Joshua could certainly sue for that back, I hated to have to tell him that he had to "elect between remedies." As a commercial landlord, he could either sue his tenant for arrears of rent or seize assets belonging to the tenant to sell to recover his rent arrears. "Seizure and sale is an old common-law remedy for commercial landlords, called distraint," I told Joshua. "The law doesn't allow you to do both." What Joshua had done by changing the locks with the heavy equipment inside was "elect to distrain." He couldn't now sue for damages (the cost of the toilet bowl, and arrears of rent).

Joshua's bewilderment at this impossible choice endeared him to me, as did his respectfulness. He had dressed up to visit me in chambers. He looked almost clown-like in his big, checkered suit with padded shoulders. Now the jacket hung off his loose frame, large even over his distended belly. He wore a bow tie and thick wartime, Groucho Marx moustache, never having changed with the times. I imagined his dancing with Marcia to big band music down at Sunnyside off Toronto's Lake Ontario shoreline. They must have cut a fine figure in their day. I could only imagine their make-up sex.

I was touched that Joshua would reach out to me as the lawyer I had become, in his hour of legal need, having watched the little girl grow up. Joshua was a jealous man, according to my father —jealous of my father's success, jealous of my father's building compared to his building, the Italian-proud upkeep, the family that grew under my father's roof, jealous of Marcia, jealous if the coffee truck guy tried to give Marcia a complimentary donut. All this couldn't have been easy for Joshua.

"Get rid of your little toilet-bowl case," my senior partner, Jack, said to me. "We've got important work to do. I need you in on this meeting."

I had Joshua in my office and the tenant and his lawyer in one of our boardrooms. Joshua probably heard my senior partner's bellowed command from reception.

I encouraged Joshua to take the $500 settlement the tenant offered and count himself lucky. The equipment pick-up was arranged for that coming weekend.

Joshua looked disappointed, but was respectful enough to take my recommendation. I wouldn't charge him for my time, I added, by way of consolation.

"Stupid," Jack hollered at me later that afternoon in the firm's reception area, in front of Jack's client, a major developer, who was too rich and important to wait for me to settle my little toilet-bowl case properly, after a respectful negotiation that didn't involve grabbing the first offer.

This is what prompted Jack's name-calling: I had taken a few precautionary moments to photo-copy a critical document in the developer's case. Jack wanted everything the instant Jack wanted it. Yesterday. The law of evidence wants the best evidence. Best evidence means the original docu-ment with original signatures. I took a few mo-ments to protect the original by photocopying it before it disappeared into the chaos of Jack's of-fice. I gave Jack the photocopy.

After Jack yelled at me in the firm's reception area, after the client left, I went into Jack's corner office. I closed the door quietly behind me. I spoke barely above a whisper—a technique I had learned from Jack, used whenever he wanted others to strain to listen, or to intimidate them.

"You will notice no one will ever hear what I am about to say to you." I had caught Jack's atten-tion. "This is because I have too much respect for you to do to you what you just did to me. You are trying to groom a firm of litigators. You are creating a firm of mice. I will never be able to work with that client before whom you have just called me 'stupid.' It took seconds, Jack, seconds, to photocopy a document I knew you would lose.

I was covering your ass." Jack said nothing. Emboldened, I continued with my Godfather whisper.

"I have found you the smoking gun in at least one case, this past year, from which you made a-quarter-of-a-million dollars. If you ever call me stupid again, I will quit, on the spot."

I slammed the door behind me.

Jack didn't come out of his office for hours.

It was a Friday night. The client in front of whom Jack had called me stupid called about 7:30 p.m. Still there, I answered the phone.

"Did I leave my briefcase there? Could you go look for it?" And then: "What are you doing, still working? What are your plans for tonight?"

I didn't get it. There never was any briefcase.

Jack said to me on the Monday: "I'll tell you who's attracted to you," and Jack named the client, now on his third divorce.

"There's this man, Zachary, I've been dating. He seems to like me."

"Hello," Jack said, "what's not to like? Just remember, it's as easy to fall in love with a rich man, as a poor man."

That will never be me, I vowed, to earn my keep on my back for some rich guy, legs in the air. Never me. Never me.

≈

Jack never called me stupid again. At least, not directly.

"I know this woman," Jack said to Zachary, when Jack was defending Zachary before the Law Society discipline tribunal, as a favour to his now junior law partner. For I had married Zachary, by then, given birth to a son. "She is an honest woman. She would never have done something as stupid as this. If you ever, ever do this to her again, you will answer to me, personally."

The 'this' was about the quick transfer of our matrimonial home from joint names into the name of the Nanny, then quick flip back into my name alone. Zachary had been the solicitor for a group of investors, acting as the lawyer on the venture and an investor, himself. Knowing the market was going to tank, that the joint venture was in jeopardy, Zachary ignored his fiduciary obligations. He conveyed his joint interest in our home to me, keeping this a secret from the other investors, who continued to invest, borrowing funds on the basis of their personal guarantees. All the joint venture participants lost their homes, except Zachary. In that, I was actively complicit. But smart for myself. Smart for our son.

"You must have gone crazy, to do something as stupid as this," Jack said. To Zachary he said: "I hear the music. Good idea at a bad time. I did it for my family. No, my friend. You did it for you. You have a serious problem."

To me, he said privately: "This man will always be trouble for you. There will be no escape, unfortunately, now that you're connected through the child."

"If you ever compromise her again, you will answer to me personally."

I was grateful to Jack for his tough words, his rough caring, for his dressing down of my careless husband. Apart from my father, Jack was the only man who had ever taken care of me. As humiliating and hard as that care had been. I owed Jack my financial life. In some ways, I owed him my life, period.

Zachary could have started all over again, walked back into a fully functioning law practice I had carried over the two months of his suspension by the Law Society. All he had to do was not repeat the same mistake. I could have started all over again, too, but never free of my obligation to Jack. Never free.

I am just outside the Law Chambers where I have laboured more than three decades. It is a Friday night. I have gone down the stairs with two heavy briefcases, purse slung over a shoulder, heading toward the curb, when the marionette cuts my strings and down I plunge, face forward, into the street. The van, heading down the street, stops, and a young man gets out, his hands shaking.

"Is my tooth bleeding?"

"No, but your nose is."

The stranger gets me wet wipes and Kleenex from the van, and I retreat to the stairs of the Law Chambers and just sit there, taking inventory. The bloody bruises on my knees blossom, my black jacket is ripped at the elbow that took the impact of my fall. I spit out the dirt of the road.

Once home, I pour myself an Epsom salts bath, and scrub away at the impact points, as my mother had done when I skinned my knees on cinders. A child of six, I had played in the dirt out the back of Joshua Bevis's building. Some of these cinders are still imbedded under my skin, some sixty years later.

Serves me right, I figure. That I should have this face plant, in front of the Law Chambers where I have served, so obediently, for over three decades. Making a buck. Selling my services. Taking the punches. Deflecting some. Everything aches, body and soul. It was my choice, of course. My choice and my fault. These raccoon eyes, the split under my right nostril. I will have to wear sunglasses on Monday. Like those battered women I have represented. Why didn't you leave? Back when he called you 'stupid' the first time? When Jack watched you struggle with his litigation brief-cases and bankers' boxes, and didn't think any-thing of it, not even when the client, embarrassed, offered to help? Jack refused the offer, for me! Jack told the client: "She's an independent woman. She'd be offended." I did speak up for myself, at least. "Actually Jack, I would not be offended. A little male chivalry might be nice, for a change." I made all my male clients carry my briefcases after that. But with that particular client, Jack overrode me. It was already too late.

The night of the fall. What am I doing here, on a Friday night, after three decades? Still work-ing for Jack?

It was only a little toilet-bowl case. But it was only ever the little toilet bowl cases about which I cared. I didn't give a shit about the million-dollar clients, though I took a Robin-Hood approach to the practice, justifying that it was the rich full-of-crap files that enabled me, a single mother, to raise my son, to work on my little toilet bowl cases. Like the logo my sign-painter father had lettered on the doors of a septic-tank truck. "Your shit is my bread and butter."

The Accidental Fugitive
(A Curious Case of Mistaken Identity)

Four policemen arrive at my door. They knock aggressively. I see them from behind my curtain and don't trust them. I, Francesca Malotti, a lawyer, do not trust in the law, or rather those with the power to administer it.

I bolt out the back door. My running convinces the authorities I am guilty.

I happen upon a family playing on their front lawn. The mother sees my distress. The family shelters me for the night. This is until they see the headlines, the next morning. There is my picture on the front page of the *Globe & Mail*: "Lawyer flees the Law." The picture they have of me is unmistakably me—the dark mane of curls flying out from either side of my head, fists pumping as I run, tight knot of exertive face, mouth open—the very picture of instinctual flight.

There is no fight left in me. I have litigated the better part of 30 years since my call to the bar. I am a member in good standing with the Law Society of Upper Canada. Yet I can barely find the breath to speak.

So, then, why do I keep taking risks — like showing up at a Chinese buffet, walking through the restaurant, about to fill my plate? Until I hear the whispers. Everyone seems to be talking about this — what I have allegedly done. I'm already condemned. I am the last person to know what this is about, or why I have fled, but knowing whatever it is, I have no chance of justice, now. Calmly, with my hunger, I leave the restaurant and discard my empty plate on a table in the outdoor patio, while a waitress looks at me, warily, as if I have stolen the best china when it is nourishment I seek. Still, no bells and whistles have gone off as I round the corner and bolt again.

I have also taken to shoplifting. The first time I do this, I am filled with exquisite delight.

There are other sightings of Francesca: On a train, trying to hide my face behind the very front page that bears my fugitive image. It is almost as if I want to be caught.

I wake from this nightmare knowing I am not the reluctant fugitive at all. For all my working life, I have been the reluctant lawyer, wanting to flee.

Lawyer by Day, Yenta by Night

Having presided over the death of so many marriages, I figure I owe it to the universe to be responsible for at least one good match. Even a divorce lawyer, hardened from toil in the vineyards of matrimonial misery, can believe that the way to human happiness is through love. *Virtutis amor*—the words on an exquisite plate from Assisi I gifted to my parents at the outset of my legal practice. Even until the end of my parents' lives, they still held hands and remained faithful in love for over 67 years. Theirs was the aspiration of what a good match can be.

But the way this match happened between Francisco and Athena wasn't deliberate on my part—at least not consciously. And some of Athena's friends, as it turns out, will never forgive me for it, though Athena forgives me and, in the throes of their exultation, she had said that she would always be grateful for everything I tried to accomplish in bringing them together. "You gave me hope."

I might have known they would ignite like firecrackers—Athena an investment broker of Greek and Macedonian background; Francisco, of Portuguese and Maltese blood. Athena is a tall, blond, gorgeous amazon of a woman with big bones and child-bearing hips, voluptuous curves, sensual lips and her casement informed by intelligence, naughty wit and imagination. Francisco is a brilliant criminal lawyer. If I could diagnose him, having learned so much from all the clinical custody and access assessment reports I'd read over 30 years of matrimonial practice, I would say he is manic, with obsessive compulsive tendencies —such as his hot-pepper phase, or Kefir phase, or juicing-his-veins-with-vitamins phase. Francisco was immediately and compulsively besotted.

It may have helped that the night of my introduction, I served Appassimento private reserve wine (vinified from carefully selected grapes and dried according to Italian tradition), fresh figs wrapped in bacon, hot pepper crostini, scallops in Pernod, veal with pasta arrabbiata. By the end of the evening, they were feeding each other, bird-like across the dining-room table.

"They'll be sucking face in the cab on the ride home," Scott said, before we ourselves were feasting on each other and dancing the horizontal lumba.

That Francisco survived his stomach cancer was attributable as much to his own obsessive-compulsive will, as to chemotherapy and the miracle of modern medicine. Prior to chemo, he'd had his sperm banked, even as he fought to remove the DNA of criminals from the data bank, all the way to the Supreme Court of Canada.

So, when I met the investment broker Athena at a charitable fundraiser, and she confessed to wanting a child, to being so sick of the men she was dating that she was contemplating purchasing the sperm of an anonymous donor, I must subconsciously have thought about my legal colleague Francisco.

"Oh, don't do that, Athena. You're so beautiful. I'm sure you will meet the right man. You are nowhere near the terminal ticks of your biological clock." I said this with authority, having had my only son at the age of 37, albeit with the wrong man, a choice I have never, by the way, regretted.

Criminal lawyer Francisco and I go back a long way. He handles all my domestic assaults. We've had some interesting cases together — like the Russian hooker case. Our mutual client, having had two previous wives and spousal and child support obligations up the wazoo, thought it would be cheaper if he simply hired sex. His mistake was bringing the Russian into his multi-million-dollar home, where she helped herself to the financial statements of his business, laying about on the desk. His other mistake was to fall in love with the hooker. But that's another story.

I actually arranged the dinner party out of revenge, to make Francisco squirm a little. This taste for revenge comes from my Sicilian (mother's blood) and Calabrian (father's blood) roots — good with the gentle insertion of the knife, then a twist. (In case you're wondering about all this mixed blood, it's pretty typical of Torontonians to have a minimum of two tributaries flowing through the veins.)

My motive was simple: Francisco had involved me in a case which went against all my better instincts and burnt us both pretty badly. Francisco, at least, got his retainer up front. My instincts were that the guy was a crook and would stiff us both for our legal fees. Francisco kept assuring me the client was good for the money, and not to worry about my retainer, he would see that I was covered. Besides, he was used to acting for guilty people. I picked my clients (stupidly, Francisco said) on the basis of belief. But my instincts were that this guy was all optics — condominium in Yorkville, rare art collection which his common-law spouse had allegedly stolen before vacating the place. I brought an injunction proceeding to the Superior Court of Ontario, family division, before learning that the Yorkville condominium squatter (not owner) had invested his common-law spouse's life savings in a Ponzi scheme and was really using his spouse's life savings to stave off the other investors. Francisco's client was taken away in handcuffs and convicted of fraud, much to the relief of the real condominium owner who'd been trying to evict him for years. Francisco and I got stiffed for thousands of dollars, I more than he, as I had given up two little "bread-and-butter" cases to handle this one big bullshit case, at Francisco's insistence. It had eaten into our friendship.

So, I decided to invite Francisco to dinner. The twist of the knife was not to let Francisco off the hook.

Scott thought it would be more fun if there was another woman at our table, and not just us three. Although the spread of years between Francisco and Athena was at least two decades, I called up Athena, the investment broker, whose card I'd kept from the fundraiser, and Athena's surprising response was "why not?" At least Athena might relate to the white-collar fraud case, about which I was determined to say nothing, unless Francisco brought it up.

For the longest time, after my dinner party, Francisco mysteriously wouldn't return my calls. Or he'd have his articling student send an e-mail to me on Francisco's letterhead, which usually began: "Ms. Malotti, this is Francisco's articling student, Antonio. Francisco would like you to give me three potential appointment times when you will be able to reach Francisco by phone. I will let you know which one is convenient to Francisco." The e-mails always ended "Faithfully yours," with Francisco's electronic signature.

Fuck you, I thought. *Your time is more valuable than mine?*

So, what I had to say to Francisco had to be said in the presence of Athena, when finally Scott called in the marker and prevailed upon Francisco to take us all out to dinner. I let it rip, bluntly.

"You owe me, buddy."

Athena had an alarmed look on her face, as if I had pimped her. (I'd have to straighten that out, later.)

"Did the Sun ever say to the Earth, 'You owe

me?' Shame on you," Francisco retorted. "That's not becoming of you, not what I'd expect from my legal sister."

"Don't go all Tao on me, Francisco. You know what I mean. If you ever break this good woman's heart, you'll answer to me personally—as in the Gucciardi brothers from Philadelphia."

"Will you give the speech at our wedding?"

"Of course, I will. When are you getting married?"

"Give me the ring on your finger, and I'll propose, right here and now."

"I'm not giving you my ring."

"Borrow then, let me borrow your ring."

"That's not the way you propose. You go out and buy something special, just like Athena is special."

Scott intervened: "Should Athena and I leave the room, so you two can brawl it out under the table? Drink up, so we can order a second bottle."

The next time I saw Athena was in a crowded room, at another fundraiser, doing the power women and networking thing. She was without Francisco. She had plumped up, as if she were on hormones, or possibly pregnant, so I asked bluntly:

"Are you pregnant?" Followed by: "When are you two getting married?" She told me, no, she wasn't pregnant but Francisco was constantly wining-and-dining her, which was making her fat. In fact, that very weekend, he was whisking her away to Portugal. So, I assumed he'd propose to her there. She wasn't sure about marriage though, it was all happening so fast, but she was having the time of her life. "Francisco is so sweet, so attentive to me, and a wonderful lover."

"What do your parents think of him?"

"My mother loves him. My Macedonian father is basically good with any man who doesn't beat me. But he is worried about the age difference."

"What's holding you back?"

"If we do have a child, it's inevitable the child will be without a father, possibly before the teen years. And I'll be of an age when it gets harder and harder to find a mate."

"So, you have a few blessed years together, then the kid inherits the earth. You inherit the earth. What can be so bad about that?"

Hold on a minute. Was I advocating? Maybe I shouldn't be trying so hard to spring Francisco's sperm out of the bank. What was happening here?

"Has your mother met Athena, yet?" I knew Francisco's mother was Francisco's deepest bond. I assumed Francisco was capable of forming other bonds based on a story he was always telling me about his pet duck. As a preschooler he'd watched the hatching of the duck, and from its first peeps out of the shell, the duck and he had bonded. It followed him to school, and when the authorities wouldn't let the duck into the classroom, it had followed him to the bus every day and was there for him upon his return.

I think they call it "imprinting." Maybe Athena imprinted on Francisco more than Francisco imprinted on her. Maybe I should have let Francisco borrow my ring.

"My mother loves Athena. But she's worried about the age difference, and she's worried about maybe Athena only wants me for my money. She wants me to have a domestic contract."

"Doesn't your mother realize shrouds have no pockets, hearses no luggage racks? Have you said anything to Athena about what your mother thinks?"

"You think I'm crazy?"

What was I doing? What had happened to my rules and personal code of conduct for matchmaking?

Rule One: Never match an executioner with a

victim. (In this case, I didn't know Athena enough to know whether she was one or the other. I knew Francisco to be an executioner, or a runner, at least through the many male-moon-walks I'd witnessed over the years. And, in any event, I hadn't really planned this one. My gut told me that Athena was an impassioned woman with no concept for "the titch principle," which my mother referred to as the rule that the man should always love the woman a "titch" more than she loved him.) They have to both be victims or both executioners. If I know that one person left their spouse for another filly in the stable, I won't set up the jilted one or the fopped one for more of the same. I will do my computer-brain thing and mix it with a little moral alignment.

Rule Two: My personal theory of all relationship breakups is that these occur because of some fundamental betrayal — whether the betrayal comes in the form of infidelity, financial, abuse (which includes substance abuse) or betrayal through too much family interference. I never match a very loyal woman with some guy who has an avowedly polygamous prick. I never pair a battered male with a controlling and abusive woman. I never set up a Mamma's boy with a fiercely independent woman.

Rule Three: Respecting the stages of the grieving process is also sacred, in my code. Therefore, I won't suggest a match between the recently wounded and someone separated for more than five years. The readiness is all, and unless the two recycled-tires are on the same rotation of the grief cycle, it's not going to work.

ᕇᕽ

That's it

"That's it."

"That's it?"

"That's it."

"What do you mean, that's it?"

"That's it, as in that's it."

"Just like that? That's it? No discussion? That's it?"

"That's it."

"So if that's it, that's it for me too. Actually, I had it in mind to say that's it before you said that's it to me."

"So agreed, then. That's it. No hard feelings."

"That's it."

Is that what this was about, then? Who got to leave who, first?

The worst of it was that neither Francisco nor Athena knew why.

What kind of man leaves a woman knowing she's pregnant with his child?

What kind of woman leaves a man knowing she's pregnant with his child?

Stating it at its most generous:

Is it because he truly loved her, enough to let her go, to find a man young and vital enough to continue with her on this journey, a man who would hold the baby in his arms from inception and be a real father to the child?

Is it because he lacked the courage for real commitment?

Is it because he knew himself to be in the last trimester of his life, she in the first, and that this reality would make the relationship impossible in the end?

Why?

Neither disclosed to the other why that was it.

Both were tortured with the not knowing.

Perhaps neither could disclose to the other why that was it.

The worst possibility was that there was no reason at all.

And what were the red flags, the warnings? Because in the not knowing, you rake back and forth across the entire relationship. Was it this?

Was it that? Did it start here, or there? Where did it begin to go wrong? Was I sleeping?

"He told me he didn't like my car. I'm not into cars. Cars are to go from here to there. I couldn't care less about a car. I suggested we buy the model he wanted. But he didn't want to buy a car. He wanted to lease. Not even a lease-to-own. A lease."

None of their friends really knew why or how it happened, either. But both of them somehow felt accountable to me. So I got their mini versions, unsolicited.

"She drank too much. She was always leaving her eye glasses and cell phone at restaurants or parties. We'd have to go back the next morning to retrieve the various bits of herself Athena left behind. It was humiliating."

"He started flirting with girls in restaurants or at parties. They could have been my nieces, some of them were so young, at least 15 years younger than me. It was humiliating."

Athena was pregnant when she and Francisco parted ways. Athena wasted no time in finding another man. The other man was 15 years older than Francisco, with connections to the Mafia.

When the baby boy was born, it was baptised and adopted into the family. *The Family*. Though the boy bore a striking resemblance to Francisco, he was given a Mafioso last name. I always thought that kind of ironic, Francisco being a criminal lawyer, and all.

Francisco paid support, faithfully, on account of his son's adoptive father. Coward that he was. But who am I to judge? After Francisco and Athena, I never tried to make another match. The urge to do what human beings can do so capably for themselves — to increase or decrease the sum total of human joy and misery — left me entirely. So that's it for this Yenta.

Pick Up Sticks

When thou dost ask me blessing I'll kneel down
And ask of thee forgiveness: so we'll live,
And pray, and sing, and tell old tales, and laugh
At gilded butterflies, and hear poor rogues
Talk of court news; and we'll talk with them
   too,—
Who loses and who wins; who's in, who's out;—
   *—**King Lear**, Act V, Sc. II*

Such a dangerous thing/To love what death can
touch.
   —Helen Spalding

You let a fistful of sticks fall. The sticks settle on the floor in a mess. The bigger the mess, the better the game. Each player tries to remove one, without disturbing the pile. The player with the most sticks at the end of the game wins.

My mother said I had "the sight." I could see how to separate one stick from another. It was uncanny. I was uncanny. Rose, my little sister, didn't stand a chance. I could play for hours, as if treading water. She hated the game. She didn't care enough to concentrate. She'd just wander off. And I didn't mind taking advantage of her inattention. Will, persistence, passion, a willingness to cheat, that's what it took. And after 10,000 obsessive games of pick-up sticks, with or without Rose—a seeming genius for it—10,000 hours being the magic number and law of mastery.

Maybe if you take the way I played into real life, it doesn't play out so well.

The night before Rose was born, I placed my head in my mother's lap. I was three, but I remember the feel of my mother's hard abdomen, the astonishing kick Rose gave to my head.

She was such a beautiful child. There is a silent home movie my father took of her in the 1950s. She is sitting on the grass in a white dress, her taffy locks neatly held back from her pretty pouting face by a large satin bow. Our parents, off camera, are attempting to coax Rose into doing something. A foot, with its frilly white sock and polished shoe, (our mother polished her daughters' shoes every night) kicks out from the dress.

"No." She will not do whatever it is they are trying to get her to do — smile for the camera, look up, come to Momma.

❧

"Fran, we got old."

My mother asked me to go to the door to retrieve her sister, my aged aunt, while she waited in the car.

Aunt Vitina's door was unlocked. In the entrance, I had been overcome by the smell of mould. Spots blossomed in my eyes. Mildew and coffee. Had she made the coffee to disguise the smell? Aunt Vitina offered me a coffee, still dressed in her coat and hat.

"No, Mom is waiting."

Outside, she fumbled at the door with the key, gave up the pretense when the door wouldn't lock. It must have been broken like this, for years.

"They can take whatever they want, even me."

I helped her into the back seat, behind the driver's seat and faced forward, when she said: "Fran, we got old."

My mother was reaching back as her sister reached forward. Their fingers touched in a palsied version of Michelangelo's creation of Adam, then laced, then slowly released, each from the other.

There is no touching now.

There were other games Rose and I had played. There was the Chinese Emperor game, with Rose holding my feet, as I read. Every now and again, I would sing an order in make-believe Chinese to keep her engaged, and she would raise or lower my feet, or put them down altogether, to bring me tea. I read a good many books in this way, with Rose as my slave. One story I remember, in particular ...

> Chi Po was a boy who drew cats. He was the youngest male child in a large, poor family, too small to help on the farm, too distracted by his doodling to be of any use. His father had given him to the monks to keep as their acolyte, thinking at least he would not starve. Though Chi Po studied and tried hard to please the monks, he could not stop himself from drawing cats. In the margins of ancient texts, on screens, anywhere he found blank spaces Chi Po drew his cats. He

drew cats because he could not really help it. Finally, the head monk called for Chi Po to be brought to him. Chi Po was destined for something, the head monk had said, but it was not to be an acolyte. Before sending Chi Po away, he gave the boy this wisdom: "Avoid the large spaces, stick to the small." Chi Po wandered for days, heading in the direction of a mountain where he knew there to be another monastery, thinking to offer himself again as an acolyte. As night approached he saw a light beckoning him, yet found the temple deserted. Chi Po was very tired, but not too tired to take out his pencils and paints, and fill the empty screens with cats. Just before he retired, he remembered the words of the head priest. "Avoid the large spaces, stick to the small." Chi Po found a small room, and inside the room, a small cupboard. He slid the cupboard door closed and let sleep embrace him. During the night there were loud howls and screeches, and thuds against walls, even to his sliding door. Chi Po lay in terror, until the howls of dying creatures ceased and the light and heat of the day made his enclosure suffocating.

Slowly, he slid back the panel to his cupboard. On the floor lay a large goblin, a monstrous rat, in a pool of its own blood. The screens Chi Po had painted the night before were still filled with his cats, now their poised claws painted red. Chi Po's fame spread throughout the land, his cats became legendary and in high demand.

Pick-up sticks remained my favourite game.

"I never had a first kiss."

My mother, hard of hearing, was fussing about the food on her sister's plate, about how my Aunt Vitina wasn't eating.

"Vitina, you eat first, and then tell us the story. Your shrimps will be cold."

I winked at my Aunt Vitina.

"Have another sip of wine, Aunt Vitina, take all the time you need."

She winked back and smacked a sip between puckered lips.

"Tastes good ... must be the company."

She let her eyes smile, the way she will do in the hospital, surrounded by her last visitors, when

I will look at her from the end of her last bed and mouth the words: "I love you." She will receive the words, close her eyes and smile, and mouth the words back to me soundlessly, her eyes bright inside a head that alone seemed alive, her body flat and still beneath the covers, as if paved to the bed. My anorexic aunt. She had only asked to be brought to hospital when she could no longer push her intestines back up her rectum.

As my mother fussed over the shrimps her sister wasn't eating, Aunt Vitina tried to tell me a story about Uncle Tony.

He was the son of the owner of a grocery store where Vitina had worked. She had been a hard worker, and Tony's mother (the grocery store owner) had thought Vitina would make her son a good wife. But there was another man who had really loved her and, as soon as Tony's mother got wind of this, Tony had thrown Vitina a ring. Literally thrown it at her, like he would later throw a diamond bracelet at his son's fiancé.

The ring had come before any kiss.

"I never had a first kiss."

"She didn't really have a honeymoon," my mother explained in the car on the way home. "There was this woman, used to work with our mother, down at Cook's Clothing. She had some rooms for let. Tony took Vitina there, and then to the tiny apartment above the fruit business. It was no honeymoon. No picnic. She got what she got. Our mother was furious. Tony had stolen her, like that. A few days later, Tony showed up at the house, when I was home, alone. He put this picture of himself in the kitchen, where our mother kept her framed photos. He just walked through the door, like he owned the place, and plunked down his picture, laughing his face off. I took it away before our mother got home. Poor Vitina. The way you start is the way you finish. She never had much of anything."

"You better tell Rose to get over there, to pick up her box. I don't think your sister has much longer to live. She must know it, to be packing her house."

At the end of our visit, my aunt gave me a statue that had stood in her hallway — a piece of statuary I'd always thought tacky but which she picked out for me, telling me it was for my beautiful bathroom. To my astonishment, it goes perfectly there, mounted beside my bathtub on an elegant wooden plant stand with slender spindle legs. The yellowed statue of the woman standing stately on one haunch has a thin veneer of drapery.

Over the woman's pelvis this veiled drapery shows her belly button, as if she has just emerged, moist from her bath, the loose-fitting gown clinging to her wet body. The sculpted woman holds a wounded bird in her arms. What yearning had Vitina felt for a life of loveliness and art?

The July I turned 10, Toronto had an awful heat wave. Rose was three years my junior. The apartment above our father's sign shop was sweltering. We were allowed to stay up later than usual. Rose and I sat on the steps of the porch above the sign shop, watching the searchlights cross the night sky, eating ice cream in our sear-sucker pajamas. Mine were blue, Rose's pink. Aunt Vitina appeared. She had come all the way from the grocery store on St. Claire Avenue, the journey taking three buses and a trolley. For all that time, she carried a box of chocolate éclairs that sat melting on her lap.

Our mother was distressed for days after. She would say things like, "Éclairs, on a hot summer night ..." and throw her dishtowel at the sink. While Rose and I ate the éclairs on the steps leading up to the porch, adult voices had drifted from the kitchen screen door, where Aunt Vitina sat with my father and mother at the table. "Gambling debt," and "if Tony doesn't pay ... we stand to lose the house."

Vitina's house was the biggest and best of all her sisters' houses. Uncle Tony loved to show up at the sign shop whenever he got a new car. He'd drive up in a Cadillac and get out, gripping a cigar between his teeth, laughing in front of our father, putting me in an arm clench. "Kid, if it weren't for your father's paint cans, he wouldn't have a pot to piss in."

While the adults talked, Rose and I ate all the chocolate éclairs.

I have never tasted such éclairs. To this day, every éclair ever after is filled with disappointment: the cream, not cream—too cold, the chocolate brittle and fake tasting. These éclairs filled my mouth with their secret pleasures, a squirting flush of warmth and sweetness. The puff of the pastry was as if I were eating the night sky, a July night never to be replicated.

"Your sister has breast cancer."

What can I possibly say? We have not spoken in years.

Not since the day I brought my unwanted

Christmas gifts over to Rose, arriving unannounced and uninvited three weeks early, a going-out-of-order in the nature of her world Rose had always hated, and met her anger with mine.

Too much was said that could not then be retracted, but could be altered and embellished to fester during the silence of the decade to follow.

What had I gone that day to say? I would not be coming to dinner, that Christmas. My son was with his father. I would be doing what I had always wanted to do, since the separation — serve meals for the homeless.

"Meals for the homeless, my ass. Charity begins at home."

"In the separation agreement, his Dad gets the play times and holidays."

"You're the mother. You're the one who should have your son on Christmas Day."

"Well, I don't. I get the work times."

"Don't give me that crap."

"So my son can work with me on his studies and music."

"It was rude — what you did last year, allowing his asshole father to pick him up, halfway through our family dinner."

"It was a privilege the kid wanted to be with both our families."

"Ruining Christmas dinner for everyone, as if the world revolves around your separation."

"A privilege—even if that meant leaving one table for another."

"Don't pull the lawyer card with me. I know what it was."

"Well, you won't have to put up with the interruption this Christmas."

"Do you think I do this for me? For me? You think I scrimp and save for months to pull off the best meal I can and slave for days in the kitchen for me? For me?"

"Well, I hope you do it for you, because if you don't do it for the joy of doing, none of your guests will enjoy it either."

This was when the really violent screaming began and where Rose started hollering about that prick-of-a-former-husband-of-mine, that now-disbarred-lawyer having fucked up the closing of their first home and was now ruining our family Christmas. Then Rose's husband came into the room and asked if this is what this was all about—my former husband? Rose's husband looked almost relieved it wasn't him. The kids, meanwhile, were quiet and hiding upstairs. Rose began screaming at her husband now too, telling him to "get the fuck out and mind your own fucking business."

"And you, you get the fuck out, too, and never come back again, don't even try to speak to me, unless it is to make an abject apology." Not just any apology, a heartfelt apology for all the wrongs I had ever done to her, and Rose would be the judge of my sincerity.

"Meals for the homeless, my ass." Rose slammed the door behind me. "You selfish bitch."

And in the intervening years, her truth, repeated so often that it must have become true, is that the insult I offered was: "You said you had never enjoyed a meal at my table."

And in all of it, there was some truth.

The meals-for-the-homeless excuse for not going to Rose's Christmas dinner was born of a roast chicken I took to our Aunt Vitina who I knew to be especially alone this time of year. Not on Christmas Day, rather several days before Christmas, and who always welcomed me with open arms, who never made me feel guilty for abandoning her for months at a time and who was grateful for the crumbs of my company, whenever these fell to her.

And it was true what Rose said about my prick-of-a-former-husband. I have no doubt that Rose and her husband were as damaged by him as was I and that they had allowed to fester whatever effect this had had upon their peace of mind or their wallets, the last of which particularly obsessed her husband.

And it was true that I had not enjoyed Christmas dinners at her house, always drinking too much and vomiting upon my return home, the result of bottled and unspoken family tensions.

And it was true that I allowed my son too many liberties, feeling he had suffered so much in the separation and because of his parents' choices that I didn't wish to make Christmas Day the battle ground of yet more suffering.

And it was true that I would rather avoid conflict where I might be asserting my parental authority, pulling the Mommy card.

But the words she put into my mouth I had not said.

I would not lie and make an abject apology for something I had not said.

"Why did she marry him when there was another?" I asked my mother, of her sister Vitina.

"I never asked ... I came home one day to find our mother hollering at Tony's mother, showing her the door. Tony's mother and my father were first cousins, from the same town in Sicily. But it wasn't about bloodlines being too close. Our mother wouldn't let Vitina return to the store. Vitina had this really nice guy courting her for months. When Tony got wind of it, next thing we know, he'd managed to put himself where he knew she would be. It wasn't for love. He wanted a good innocent girl who'd wait on him hand and foot. Young and stupid ... easily manipulated. They eloped the day he proposed and the rest is the rest ... I never asked. She never told."

～

"Your sister has breast cancer."

We are in a rowboat, surrounded by islands. I am rowing, without direction or bearings. The way dreams release information, I know the islands are floating—their vegetation dangling rootless in the water, like so many disengaged lily pads. And then we lose an oar. I use the rescuer's dive where hands come together, just beneath the surface of the water like closing wings, and legs and feet scissor below water in opposite directions, keeping my head above, sights on the oar. I swim to retrieve it. Being a strong swimmer, I have no doubt about my ability to reach it. But when I grasp the oar and pivot in the water, I see I have now lost the boat. I see the look in her eyes as my sister drifts away. There is too much watery space between us—a chartless infinity of shifting islands. She drifts away, alone. I feel my sister's horror and know I am responsible. I cannot rescue her ...

We have not spoken in years.

"You need to do this for your mother," I say to my almost adult son, Marco.

I have returned home after my own breast examination. The mammogram: everything seems to be clear. I wonder how many times during her suffering did Rose ponder Why me? Why not my sister? I pass by my house on the way downtown to work. My son, having completed first year chemical engineering, hasn't thought yet about a summer job. He is sleeping off his exams. It is about 11 in the morning. He hauls himself out of bed for this urgent mission requested by his mother. To think of the time we have lost!

"I have to make a call," I tell Marco. "I can't do this and drive. I must do this, now. You'll have to take me downtown. I'm sorry you have to hear this."

Marco pulls on track pants, flips up the hoodie. He doesn't bother with shoes and socks, slips his bare feet into slippers. Looking ghetto were it not for me in the passenger seat of the Lexus, the police would definitely be hauling him over.

"I did call," I tell Rose. "Three times, I tried. You never picked up the phone. And then, one day, there was an answering machine. When I tried to leave a message, I heard the phone pick up and down, the dial tone ..."

Rose has started to cry. I am crying too.

"All the time I was going through chemo, I just wanted to hear ... Just hear you ask—even once ... How was I? How was my day?"

"I was afraid ... I thought even the sound of my voice might disturb your healing."

"... Just to hear, that you loved me ..."

We arrive at the office. My son opens the car door. He takes my briefcase and the box of Kleenex, guides me up the stairs of the underground car park, then up the stairs of the Old Soddy. It is 11:20 in the morning. We are the only ones in the bar. The waitress brings us both a scotch, which my son has apparently ordered, and popcorn, before I realize where we are.

"What if somebody sees us?"

"Nobody, but nobody, from your office is going to see you here."

He sits there, waiting, in his slippers and hoodie, for me to take the first sip.

The box had been sealed. The box Aunt Vitina meant for Rose, her goddaughter. It had her name written across the top in Aunt Vitina's shaky script, written just a few months before her death. I knew it must be filled with small treasures, as Rose always got the best presents for her birthday, for Christmas, all special occasions, and even in between, for no reason at all, like the chocolate éclairs. Aunt Vitina took being a godmother seriously, and showered Rose throughout her life. It would be no different in death.

"Tell your sister to come, to come soon. I want to see her open this," Aunt Vitina said of the box, so carefully prepared for her goddaughter.

But Rose never got there. Vitina's daughter brought the box to Rose after her mother's death.

"It was opened before I got there," the daughter explained to Rose. "I didn't open this."

Inside, there was one chipped china teacup hastily re-wrapped. What else had there been? What especially became of that ring—the ring Aunt Vitina promised to Rose, the ring Uncle Tony had thrown to her, before any kiss?

"I never had a first kiss."

I am doing laundry in my empty house, my only son long gone. There is no reason for me to keep the house now, other than an unwillingness to let go, to admit the time for my big house has passed. I reach into the basket of hangers I keep in my laundry room to hang the half-dry clothing in the open doorways of my empty bedrooms. I try to untangle the cleaners' hangers. In my impatience, I pull a pile onto the floor. Some get caught in the holes of the laundry basket. Some settle on the floor in a mess. I end up on my hands and knees, yanking at hangers, turning the basket upside down, taking it out on the hangers, whatever it is. No cheating now. No time left for games.

I have finally lost at pick up sticks.

"I love you, Rose."

Too little. Too late.

"And how was your day? Are you doing your laundry? How fares my little sister? How fares my Rose?"

My House of Many Rooms

Give her of the fruit of her hands;
and let her own works praise her in the gates.
  —*Proverbs 31:31*

My house was built on what used to be the fifth hole of the Humber Valley Golf Club, high on a hill. There is a great maple tree in the backyard. There used to be a huge willow at the back fence, until its branches began to fall, one destroying a neighbour's fence. I had to have the willow taken down, the cut at its base so deep it hurt. The arborist levelled it, as best he could. It was the size of a dinner table, upon which I displayed my son's discarded trucks, now covered in growth.

From the front bedroom windows, I can still see the Humber River beyond the houses across Stonegate Road, the ravine and forest beyond. When I first opened the balcony doors off the master bedroom, Canada geese flew overhead. Whenever a city siren sounds during the night, wolves howl from the Humber spit. A fox has paused, Sphinx-like, in one of my flowerbeds. I have surprised a male buck, scratching its antlers against the mulberry tree.

"You must take care of this piece of God's earth," one of my friends said who lay dying. Unable to bring my friend to the garden, I brought the garden to him, in the form of a picture — my last gift.

This house was built on hallowed ground in the year of my birth, 1952.

I had an Uncle Joseph who died well before then, reportedly of a broken heart, in the Dirty Thirties. I know he had walked over my lands. He had played golf before any Italian immigrant heard of the game. Now Italian developers own golf courses as a badge of their financial arrival. Uncle Joseph had also belonged to the Humber River Canoe Club and had paddled the waters beyond the houses across the street, the ones with riparian rights, at a time when there was no Stonegate Road, at a time when his Calabrian parents who had not known how to swim could neither comprehend nor endorse his leisure pursuits. In the only picture I have of him, Uncle Joseph looks like the Great Gatsby. He had dreams, had tried to fly as far as his wings could stretch.

I live on sacred ground.

High on the hill across the ravine in back of my house there is a stone carved in commemoration to Étienne Brûlé, the first European explorer to have gazed upon Lake Ontario from a nearby spot. It is dedicated to all adventurous spirits to have passed this way.

Indigenous peoples walked over this land, this little piece of God's earth. When I dig into my garden, I hear them exhale. Everything is borrowed, even our own time.

How fiercely I fought for this home to save it from a charming, venal husband and his creditors — standing between these wolves and my one only son.

My home.

My garden.

"Do you have a daughter, sir?" I asked my cross-examiner, in one of my husband's lawsuits, when questioned about the transfer of title into my name. "Then you don't need to ask that question. I'd have walked through fire for the sake of my son. God help your daughter, should she ever marry a man like my husband, and have a creditor the likes of your client at her door."

My cross-examiner turned pink, as did my own counsel. I was told, afterward, I made a terrible witness. However terrible, I defeated the fraudulent preference allegation. As if a wife can be on a par with general creditors! I managed, somehow, to keep my home. My house, high on a hill above the river, swept by wind, but safe from flood. My little piece of God's earth. A temporary license. A brief season of safety.

To the father: "I'll be God damned if I'm going to feather yours and her love nest, or that it should go to your creditors. At least if I hold title, it will go to our son."

To the son, when the time came for him to know: "When I die, you stand to inherit the earth."

How ridiculous, our human laws of property, that it is ever permitted "to have and to hold," to death or any other parting.

At this terrible time of defending my home, I had dreams of another, of rooms in which I had never lived and of a woman not of my time—a woman in long skirts whose shoes stepped hard across bare wooden floors. Her family had waited in a wagon as the Zulus came for them. She went through each of her rooms. I saw these rooms, from the vantage of her knees, leaning against her skirts, as if I might have been the youngest child she took on this last tour with her, saw the capable hands that straightened the sheets, smoothed the covers and tucked every corner. When the enemy entered they would find everything in perfect order. She did this before a certain violation, her family waiting. She did this without fear, with utmost patience that would not be rushed, closing each door behind her. They would arrive, bewildered, not knowing what to make of these beds, how to violate the woman who wasn't home, who had made them all wait, just before her leave-taking in her own time.

Did she make it this woman?

Did it matter?

I would wonder with every waking after this dream.

I knew that her trauma had mysteriously preserved itself for me, given to me in my own time, so I would know how to behave in the face of my own enemies.

I would lay a table.

I would stand my ground.

I would vacate and give way, only when my own time came to heed the cry of the Zulus.

I would take with me the vision of my rooms, just as I had left them, in pristine condition. I could let go with that knowledge and in peace. I had worked hard. I had taken care of that which I loved. I had taken care of my little borrowed piece of God's earth.

Pasta With The Priests
(Miracle on Bond Street)

Father Mercutio invites Francesca Malotti to dinner with the priests. "Maria's tuna pasta is a rectory favourite." Since the rectory is right next door to the Law Chambers where Francesca works, the only female lawyer among "10 angry men" as she fondly calls her male partners, this is a convenient invitation. Besides, Wednesday nights her son spends with his father.

Her first encounter with Father Mercutio was shortly after his arrival at the Choir School. Not knowing his way around the buildings, Father Mercutio managed to trap himself in a rarely-used corridor, closed off due to water damage the Choir School could not afford to repair. When the corridor door clicked behind him and the door onto Bond Street would not open, Father Mercutio thought he would be trapped in this inner corridor indefinitely. So, he panicked, as if he himself were one of the frightened little choir-boys. Father Mercutio banged on the door and cried for help. Going down on his knees, he opened the mail flap with his small fingers and saw a woman in a circle of people speaking animatedly with her hands, as in a Duccio mural. She looked back over her shoulder toward the sound of his cries and left her group, still speaking, casually grabbed the door handle and tugged hard. To Father Mercutio's relief, the door opened to her vigorous yank and they both laughed at his embarrassing predicament—a priest on his knees, begging for help.

It turned out she had a son at the Choir School.

Death by Popcorn

There are some duties even the most dedicated of priests can find unbearable. The worst, Father Mercutio tells Francesca Malotti, over wine the night of pasta with the priests, are the daily confessions of those without real sins. He tells Francesca this after he, the Deacon and Francesca retire to a study overlooking Bond Street with the remains of the Ripasso wine Francesca has brought to the feast. The Deacon, a seminarian studying for the priesthood, sits like Humpty Dumpty on a chair with one diminutive leg folded under his enormous and egg-shaped abdomen, sipping discerningly as Father Mercutio, himself a small man no taller than most of the choirboys he teaches, tells Francesca about these "sinless confessions" in answer to her question about the "worst part of being a priest."

"You recognize the voice you heard yesterday, and the day before that — the litany of petty wrongs. I suspect these people come to confession just to hear another human voice. For the priest, listening to these types of confessions, well, it's death by popcorn."

The Deacon laughs with operatic hilarity and Francesca joins in, though she feels uncomfortable at the irreverence of their laughter in relation to what is supposed to be a sacrament. The healing that is supposed to come when, overcoming our fears, we admit our wrongs to God and to ourselves. She tries to imagine how excruciatingly long it would take to die that way and to empathize with the priests who have to hear "trivial" confessions, those persons who come daily to unburden themselves, if only to hear their own voice and the response of another human being.

"Every now and then, you get a really good confession that makes up for all the popcorn."

Francesca's first confession, after years of abstinence from the Catholic Church, had been prompted by her lover. Her lover was a former hockey player who had himself come up through the Catholic ranks, but not spiritually — rather, skating it out with the other jocks at St. Michael's on Bathurst Street in Toronto, toughened by the Basilian fathers. "Get up, get up," the Basilian fathers had yelled over him as Francesca's now lover had to her boy, when Marco fell to the ice and just lay there. It was Francesca's lover, her sweet and secret sin, who admonished her to "get your ass over to the Catholic Church and fill in those envelopes, make yourself known, so your boy can take his first communion." This was not something Francesca ever shared with Father Mercutio, nor any priest, unable to feel her love for this man or his love for her could possibly be sin. Did Mary Magdalene feel similarly silenced around the apostles?

"Bless me father, for I have sinned. It has been about 10, well, actually maybe 20, years since my last confession … In fact, I don't think I will be able to make a full confession. You have a long line-up outside and the Mass is about to begin."

It was just before Easter, the morning of

Good Friday, and her last opportunity for confession if she hoped to take the host on Easter Sunday. But divorced Catholics are not supposed to take the host. Some real Catholics suffer over this. But Francesca wasn't a "divorced" Catholic. Her first marriage had been annulled making Francesca an "annulled" Catholic. Her second marriage was in the Anglican Church, and that, according to one priest, wasn't a real marriage in the eyes of the Catholic Church. So, technically, she wasn't a divorced Catholic and could still take communion if she had been able to buy into the bullshit of what was real and what wasn't real. To be honest, Francesca didn't give a damn about the ability to take communion in the Catholic Church. But for some mysterious reason she did give a damn about her son's ability to do so.

"Don't you worry about the line-up, dear, you take all the time you need," the anonymous priest in the confessional of St. Michael's Cathedral said on that Good Friday. Her heart sank. How was she to start up that mountain of her life again?

"Spit it out, woman," her lover had said to her when she had tried to tell him about the two former husbands ...

Cutting to the quick, there was the choice of her first husband — the charismatic, handsome Paolo Giovanazzo who turned out to be an abuser.

Francesca had been a virgin on their wedding night. Having come from loving parents, she didn't understand that a man could say he loved you and yet be so cruel—hate everything you were and loved. She had been a student of music, at the time, studying voice at the Royal Conservatory of music—he, an engineer. Only 19 years of age, Francesca hadn't yet found a way of being in the world. Spending most of her days in the cloistered world of the Conservatory, inside a private studio practising hours a day when other girls her age were out partying, drinking, having sex, burning bras, attending protests, she had little experience of men nor what kind of men to avoid. She had thought, by marrying Paolo, that he would be her way of being—a traditional choice, of which her Italian parents had approved. After marriage, she would simply continue with her passion and her gift—the voice she had been given at birth and had a responsibility to cultivate. The voice Paolo hated. He hated her voice because it took her away from him. The first time he penetrated her, he pinned her wrists above her head, stopped her mouth with his free hand and spread her legs with his knee.

"The Catholic Church annulled that marriage, Father, at the instance of my abuser. He used the legal argument I was unwilling to bear children. That was a lie. This lie turned me away from the Church—that my marriage had to be void *ab initio*. The Church turned me into a whore on my wedding night, which is what he called me—whore. And worse.

"I was fortunate in the love of my good parents. This love enabled me to escape. The marriage ended after only three months. Many years after that, years of floundering, I entered law school. I never sang again."

Francesca paused. So how, now, to fast forward?

"After 10 years of recovery, I met and married my son's father. This was my second real sin."

The sin of this second marriage, to the man who would eventually become her son's father, was that she had married Zachary without love. Francesca had married Zachary knowing she didn't love him, married him for the wrong reason—fear of loneliness. And when she realized she could not continue in the loveless marriage, with an attachment that truly was void from the beginning, she had gotten out.

Because she had married Zachary in the Anglican church, it wasn't a real marriage according to one priest she had consulted. Francesca had argued with that priest: "What does that make of my son? Doesn't that make him a bastard? No,

Father, it was a real marriage. The child born of that marriage is a real child."

Francesca's sin is also real—conceiving a child to a loveless marriage. There would be lifelong and real repercussions for the son. Now that she had left his father, Marco would never have any siblings, had to shuttle back and forth between two houses, always in conflict with himself; having to watch his mother always in conflict with herself, her voice now used in the service of greedy warring people who hired that voice only to spout their one-sided truths, which she did convincingly for mammon, to stave off the wolf at the door, so that she could keep want away from her son—this treasured son, whom she loved more than any being in the world.

"It comes down to two sins, Father," she told the anonymous priest, summing things up in her closing argument, like the lawyer she had become. "The sin of not honouring my gift. The sin of conceiving a son to a loveless marriage. And for these sins, but especially the second of these, I am most heartily sorry."

Francesca came to the end of her confession. All out of breath, there was a long pause—she dreaded to hear what was at the end of that silence. What came out of the darkness and silence was a surprise. The priest told her that she must not confuse the agents of the Church with the one true God. And then: "God loves you. He has given you many gifts. For your penance, I want you to sing one Glory Be to God, and to sing this prayer in the morning, in the privacy of your own room, first thing upon waking. Answer the invitation of the Gloria. Do you remember the words?" And astonishingly, the priest, quietly at first and then with rising passion, began to sing the words for her recall, sing—contrary to the cannon law no singing during Lent—sing from his compartment of the confessional such that when Francesca left the confessional booth, having been granted absolution, free to guide her own son to his own first confession and communion, her face was hot with humility and grace:

> Glory to God in the Highest and
> Peace to his people
> On earth
> Lord God
> Heavenly King
> Almighty God and Father
> We give you thanks
> We worship you
> We praise you for

His Glory
Lord Jesus Christ
Only son of the Father
Lord God
Lamb of God
You take away the sins
Of the World
Have mercy on us
You are seated at
The Right hand of the Father
Receive our Prayer
Glory to God in the highest and
Peace to his people
On earth
For you alone
Are the holy one
You alone are the Lord
You alone
Are the most high
Jesus Christ
With the Holy
Spirit in the Glory
Of God the Father
Glory to God in the Highest and
Peace to his people
On earth.

Six Bottles of Ripasso

Francesca carries six bottles of assorted Ripasso wines in a box down the stairs of her Bond Street Law Chambers and over to the door of the building where the choirboys hold their practices and where Father Mercutio meets her at the Principal's office. Together, they deposit the box in the room where they will be dining, at a long table which seats 12, and Father Mercutio takes Francesca on a backstage tour of the Choir School. Here are the rooms where seminarians or priests from foreign jurisdictions stay while visiting Toronto, and there is the corridor where Father Mercutio became stuck the day Francesca rescued him. Not making the same mistake twice, Father Mercutio holds the interior door open and points to the outside door. The stairwell echoes its disuse, but has amazing acoustics as Father Mercutio demonstrates by singing a few bars. He tells her he had gone there, the day they met, to practice in privacy.

Francesca is particularly fascinated by the cloistered area with stained windows above the auditorium — a cozy Victorian interior lined with books and stacked with music scores and a dusty assortment of wingback chairs and Jacobean straight-backs, unused fireplace, and lead-plated windows that open out onto Bond Street. It must be from these windows that Francesca hears the boys practising, year after year, as springtime blossoms toward summer.

"It's magical when snow falls onto Bond Street at night, capping the street lights. You know the movie, *Miracle on 42nd Street*? Well, there should be a Miracle on Bond Street, because that's what we've got here, a little miracle."

Back downstairs in the basement dining room, Maria, already busy over the pasta pot, refuses Francesca's offer of assistance.

The diners quickly assemble at the appointed time. All men. And although all have received advance warning of Francesca's attendance, all are uncomfortable as is she. The configuration at table is a blur. Four of the men who face her could be labourers at work somewhere in the bowels of the St. Michael's complex. Francesca has never seen any of them before. Respectfully cleaned up for dinner, they wear blue jeans, white undershirts with sweaters over top, looking distinctly European and celibate. Throughout dinner they never speak a word, keeping their faces bowed over their plates—though, when Francesca offers each a glass of wine, they exchange glances between themselves before accepting.

Seated at the head of the table is the most

distinguished in their midst. Although he wears a simple priestly collar, his left hand bears a ring. Francesca cannot remember being introduced, though she must have been. Perhaps she is simply expected to know who he is. Unto him is given the task of saying grace. When all the plates are down in front of each diner, heads bowed, the head priest says grace.

"Bless us, O Lord, and these, Thy gifts, which we are about to receive from Thy bounty. Through Christ, our Lord. Amen."

It is the standard Catholic grace, pronounced in a perfunctory manner, no flight of creativity allowed for any departure, as rote as the sign of the cross that precedes and follows it, before they tuck into their tuna pasta.

To the distinguished priest's left sits the Deacon-becoming-priest. In her confusion, Francesca promptly forgets his name, but identifies him in her mind's eye as Humpty Dumpty because of his oddly stunted legs beneath his enormous egg-like abdomen.

Then comes Father Mercutio, and to his left, Francesca. The chair to Francesca's left remains empty.

Thankfully, Francesca has thought to bring wine and told Father Mercutio that she would be doing so. Humpty Dumpty carries the day with his ebullient welcome and enthusiasm over each bottle, deciding to uncork all six, at once, without seeking anyone's permission, so that all can breathe and be sampled. He knows his stuff, commenting on the subtle differences between bottles. The wine and Maria's pasta are the main topics of conversation. Maria clearly appreciates being appreciated, particularly by Humpty Dumpty whose plate Maria keeps full, without asking. But that she disapproves of Francesca is obvious.

The sampling, at first, takes place in small quantities. Francesca offers to rinse glasses between tastings. As she goes back and forth into the kitchen to rinse a glass, each individually, so as not to confuse glasses and tasters, Maria's body language resists her. Francesca tries to encourage Maria to share in the wine tasting, but Maria will not. Nor does Maria sit at their table, although she will attend to it including offering seconds when the time comes to offer seconds. Maria will not let Francesca participate in serving up the plates of pasta, which she serves, individually and quickly.

Francesca looks around at the various table settings, the unmatched cutlery and mixed silverware, the chipped plates and assortment of glasses and crystal, none of which come from the same pattern — a wondrous variety composed from other kitchens, other households, other lives.

What are they celebrating? Why has Father Mercutio asked her to pasta with the priests?

First Gifts

Francesca has found a way of being in the world and is successful at it in the ways of the world. She has a boy at the Choir School. This is the unspoken preamble to some request she knows is coming, and come it does — directly after dinner, in the small Victorian sitting room above Bond Street to which Francesca, Father Mercutio and the Deacon retire with the remains of the wine.

Would she be the benefactress of a Christmas Carol specifically written for St. Michael's Choir School?

What a wonderful idea!

So, they begin to converse about the essence of an enduring Christmas Carol. Francesca has her own favourite precedents: What Child is This, I Saw Three Ships, and her favourite of all time, the English 16th century Coventry Carol. It is the simplicity of the lyrics wedded to the music — a simplicity which echoes the humbleness of the birth in a manger, the nakedness with which we are born and die. We come from a silence before the womb into a hollering, cacophonous, terrifying, confusing, harmonious, mystical, evil, glorious world and, no sooner sung and cadenced, return to silence again.

The evening ends with a knock at the Victorian sitting-room door. Father Mercutio answers still holding a wine glass in his hand. Francesca hears him giving some guidance on a repair that workmen had volunteered to do, after hours. Humpty Dumpty has long ago stopped talking and is snoring loudly from his chair, his little hands entwined, fingers folded clerically above his stomach. His empty glass is at the foot of his chair, tucked safely beneath, like one practiced at avoiding spillage.

"That couldn't have looked very good," Father Mercutio says to Francesca, just before they adjourn for the night, "a priest answering the door with a glass of wine in his hand." To say nothing of the woman in the room, their chaperone asleep.

On the cab ride back to her empty home, knowing her son is exercising his infrequent access to his father that night, Francesca mulls over the commission, which she will fund.

First Gifts
(A Christmas Carol in 4/4 time)

The first time ever I see your face
I weep at your nativity
I see the babe with hands up-reached,
I see the man with arms outstretched.

Alleluia, Alleluia, Alleluia.

I feel your face with little hands
I taste the salt of your fears
I taste my own humanity,
Swaddled in a love of tears.
Alleluia, Alleluia, Alleluia

What can I give this babe of mine?
With straw for bed, and roof so low?
What can I do for him divine?
That he himself knows not to sew?

Alleluia, Alleluia, Alleluia.

The first time ever I hear your voice
I seek you with these eyes so blind,
Your song first heard from inside
Sound of Mother Creator mine.

Alleluia, Alleluia, Alleluia.

I see the lamb yet to be,
Rejoice for all humanity.
My peace, my love, I give to you
My love for all eternity.

Alleluia, Alleluia, Alleluia.

Priests in Reception

"Francesca," the receptionist announces through the phone, "there are two priests for you in reception. They said they do not have an appointment."

The receptionist sounds surprised. Usually, when Francesca gets a call like this it is two officers in uniform who want to see her. Once it was to tell her a client had been murdered. Although the building that houses the Law Chambers is proximate to the Cathedral, no one has ever had any experience of priests in the reception area. And what priest would have occasion to consult with a matrimonial lawyer?

As luck would have it, Francesca is having a desk day, not required to be in court, and is available.

It is Father Mercutio and the Deacon, Humpty Dumpty.

"What an unexpected surprise." Francesca greets them and leads them toward her office. Father Mercutio says he has never been in a Law Chambers before, and looks around with such curiosity that Francesca decides to give them a little tour — here the library, right across from her individual office, there the lunch room, where her son, Marco, brings a few of his buddies after school for hot chocolate in the winter, while he waits for his mother to clean up her desk so they can leave for the day. (She doesn't tell them about the inter-office memo one of her partners sent around, that the hot chocolate is for clients only, over which Francesca threatened to resign her partnership unless the partner retracted his pettiness, which led to quite a stir among the 10 angry men.)

She shows them the view from her window, which looks into the now silent Choir School playground (it is summer break), and where she has watched in horror her son whaling on some kid in a circle of boys on his first day at the Choir School. Her boy entered the Choir School in grade five, after friendships and cliques were well established, and when one of the boys had challenged him, her son knew instinctively that if he didn't beat-the-shit out of that kid, then and there, his days at the Choir School were doomed. She doesn't tell the priests this. Rather, she tells them what a joy it is to be able to bring her son a second set of mittens when his have gone missing, or her own lunch, when he has somehow misplaced his lunch box or had it stolen, that without her son being at the Choir School, Francesca doubts she could have continued in the practice of law, as a single mother.

Then Francesca sits behind her desk and indicates the two client chairs where the priests settle. She comes to the point,

"What can I do for you?"

Father Mercutio takes out from his breast pocket two handwritten sheets of music, which he unfolds neatly on her desk. From another pocket, he takes out a tuning pipe, from which he sounds a note. Then Father Mercutio and Humpty Dumpty lean forward, and begin to sing acapella and in counterpoint the voice of Mary and the voice of the Christ Child, and when they come to the words—

Your song first heard from inside
Sound of Mother Creator mine—

Francesca bursts into tears.

Do they hear it? Do they hear what she hears? Does Father Mercutio know how anarchic that is? She has named the Creator Mother. Not Father. Not our Father in Heaven, hallowed be thy name. This is an intimate and loving duet between the child and his mother, a mother and her child. It is full of wonder and fear, the miracle of life and love.

Truth be told, in the business of getting on with everyday life, the winning and losing, the whaling on the bullies as a daily act of survival, Francesca has forgotten all about her Christmas carol. She can scarcely believe she has written these words or commissioned the words be set to music. She has taken the mammon of her clients, clean and unclean, and turned her 30 pieces of silver over to the priests of St. Michael's, over to one priest, in particular, so that they, so that he could make a heavenly noise of it, with the choir of raucous school boys in which sings her very own son.

"My sacrificial lamb," she jokingly refers to Marco. "I will not ask you to do anything I would not do with you." She has promised him this from the time he auditioned for the Choir School and has been true to her word. They have lived through three liturgical years of mass, together.

She has even arranged to cab her son all the way from Brampton to downtown Toronto whenever her former husband, Marco's Anglican father, refuses to drive him. (He told their son it was all his mother's fault, his loss of his driver's license when his car was impounded for driving while under suspension—never acknowledging any responsibility—that it was for his own non-payment of child support for which his license was suspended.) So Francesca and son have kept up the mass commitment together, while her son gets a musical education at the Choir School, culminating with the crucifixion and resurrection of Christ and beginning all over again on Christmas Day. And when she sees the rows of saintly boys, their little shoulders shaking, Francesca knows some horseplay is up behind the altar, will find out later what has made the boys giggle—"Daniel farting a D below middle C"—identified by Zaddi, who has perfect pitch.

It is so simple. The miracle. What goes into an enduring Christmas carol. What makes it a miracle. Community. Being part of a choir. Love.

Joso's

To thank Father Mercutio for setting her words to music, Francesca invites him for lunch at Joso's

—an upscale Toronto eatery near the corner of Avenue Road and Davenport, with an intriguing seafood menu, including squid-ink-infused pasta, and an even more intriguing interior, inspired by the Dalmatian coast, artwork Francesca has forgotten about until her arrival that day for lunch.

Francesca used to go to Joso's frequently with her crazy criminal lawyer colleague who handled all her domestic assaults. She had forgotten about the paintings. Many of these were accomplished by the owner chef who enjoyed his naked wife in versions of the goddess Minerva and other provocative subjects from ancient mythology. Francesca assumed these athletic couplings also featured self-portraits of the chef.

Francesca arrives at the restaurant early and sees that their table-for-two has been reserved in front of a particularly salacious painting. Seeing the restaurant for the first time through the eyes of a priest, she enlists the wife's assistance to suggest a more appropriate positioning of the priest, help shepherd him immediately to the appointed seating arrangement, basically facing a dark interior with his back to the door. When Father Mercutio arrives, Francesca apologizes profusely for her choice of venue.

"No mind," he says, "the priests back at the rectory warned me. I've seen worse at the Vatican."

At that, Father Mercutio tells her the story of having dined at the Vatican and studying one particular painting all through lunch which he thought had been ruined by water damage or sloppy painters working overhead. In a moment of revelation, he realized the dribbles of vertical whiteness were the artist's rendition of lactating mothers.

"I always thought that an unusual choice of art for the Pope's dining room, but on the other hand, oddly appropriate."

They both laugh and get down to the business of ordering lunch.

"How so?" Francesca then asks, while they are waiting for their order to be brought. "How, appropriate?"

"Well, either the baroque artist had a sense of humour, or the Vatican curator who situated this particular piece in the dining room. But I also think it was there to tell us to be mindful of something."

"What's that?" Francesca asks.

"Where we all got our first meals."

~e~

Is it possible the anonymous priest who received her confession that day—the day that led to her son's first communion, to her son becoming a choirboy at St. Michael's, to pasta with the priests, to the gift of a Christmas carol, to the miracle on Bond Street—might have been Father Mercutio? From time to time over the years of their friendship, Francesca Malotti wonders, but then immediately dismisses the idea. Impossible. That priest had been a much older man, a man who called her "dear." Surely Francesca would have recognized his voice? The anonymous priest of the confessional who sang the Gloria had been a baritone. Father Mercutio is a tenor.

Francesca might never have wondered again if Father Mercutio hadn't asked her a question. The question resonates long after the meal of pasta *alla pescatore* has ended.

"Have you got back to singing? Have you used your own voice, again—the voice that God gave you? Have you sung any Gloria, lately?"

EPILOGUE

Surrender

'Let me not live,' quoth he
'After my flame lacks oil, to be the snuff
Of younger spirits . . .'
*—**All's Well That Ends Well**, Act 1, Sc. II*

I didn't expect to weep after I pressed the SEND button on my Surrender Application. What was I surrendering? I thought it was my licence to practice law. It surprised me, how much I cried, uncontrollably, for hours—sobbed, in fact, as I hadn't in many years of grieving over the deaths of my father, my mother, my senior law partner . . . And now I was grieving something I hadn't expected to grieve—myself as a barrister, a lawyer. I hadn't realized how much I had grown to value the role symbolized by the robes, how much the law had anchored me, formed the ostinato base over which all the melodies of my life had played.

I had always believed my ego was little invested in "being a lawyer," that I had gone into law reacting to something my mother had said. Mom had watched from the sidelines as I floundered too long on the threshold of adult life, had admonished me one day with exasperation: "Why don't you make something of your life, like your friend Irene?" My friend Irene happened to be a lawyer. So I wrote the LSAT as a walk-in, on a kind of dare, without any preparation. If I could not do what I thought I really wanted to do, in my heart of hearts, then at least I could achieve at a mediocre level, or so I thought at the time — do something that would burn up the hours like a match to human hair, make writing impossible, make me let go of my failed dream.

Surrender. What does it mean to surrender?

The Oxford English Dictionary gives many definitions, the most common of these involves handing over of property, relinquishing possession on compulsion or demand, giving in to another's power or control, accepting an enemy's demand for submission. My eye lights on this one: "give oneself up; cease from resistance; submit." And a more figurative use: "To give oneself up to some influence, course of action, etc.; to abandon oneself or devote oneself entirely to ..."

Surrender. What a powerful word.

What did it mean to me, to have such a powerful effect?

I practised law for 35 years, 40 if you include my legal education, articles, and the bar admission course that preceded active private practice.

As a litigator, I became aware of the power of words early in my legal career. The first time I stood up in what was then called Weekly Court (where appeals from civil procedural motions were heard), I was told by the Judge that he did not need to "hear" from me. "But, My Lord," I said. "There are things I need to say." I felt a tug on my gown from behind. When I turned, the senior silk behind me was mouthing: "Sit down. It means you've won." I had "won" on the basis of my factum, my written statement of fact and law.

Another experience that stands out concerned a very lengthy pleading and affidavit I'd written on behalf of a mother who was bringing an emergency custody application before the Court. The mother believed her four-year-old child to be at risk in the care of his abusive father. She feared if she left out anything, that omission might result in the failure of her case. We couldn't take that chance. The need to say it all and urgently resulted in many hours of drafting. I admittedly went overboard. My pleading was not limited to the "material facts," without supporting evidence, as a

pleading is supposed to do. My pleading ex-
pressed the fear in the voice of the child. In a
non-partisan reach-out, which was all about pro-
tecting the child, I had asked opposing counsel
to arrange to serve the father in his office the day
before the emergency application, the day the
mother withheld access. When we appeared in
judge's chambers, the next day, opposing counsel
brought a very partisan motion to strike my pleading as "embarrassing and prolix," which I readily
conceded. But only after winning the intended
result. "I couldn't put the pleading down," the
Judge said. "I felt this mother's pain." The power
of words.

To advocate — to speak for, to give voice to
those who otherwise would not have a voice. The
best work I have ever done as an advocate did this
— give voice to the pain of others and let them
tell their stories so that others could listen and
really hear. Being a porous human being, being
someone who also cared, I absorbed the pain.

After four decades, I surrendered.

When I discussed the various options with the
Law Society Information Officer, I asked: "Isn't
surrender sometimes offered to a lawyer as an alternative to being disbarred, to having one's license irrevocably revoked? Can't the Law Society
use the word retire instead of surrender, in the

case where a lawyer comes to the decision she will never practice again, after an unblemished career?" The Information Officer was very uncomfortable with the question, and basically invited me to do my own research by referring me to the By-law. The alternatives offered to surrendering my licence: "If you are 65 years of age (or older), or at any age if you are incapacitated and unable to practice law, you may qualify for exemption from the requirement to pay the Law Society annual fee and submit the Law Society annual report if the standards set out in subsections 4(1)-(5) of By-Law 5 and subsections 5(3)-(8) of By-Law 8 are satisfied."

Who was I kidding? I knew I would never practise again. What was the point of deferring the decision?

After decades of thinking myself a good or bad person, largely based on whether I "won" or "lost," where the best news I ever got to deliver mostly consisted of "You're divorced," I had a diagnosis of "complex grieving issues," "situational depression" and "post-traumatic-stress disorder" (PTSD). I had clawed my way back from these, stepped back from the brink. I was enjoying a modest practice after the rigors of downtown practice and partnership when COVID hit. But the reasons, the real reasons went deeper than any of these.

I didn't want to practise, ever again. I had lost all desire, all lust for the fray.

And yet, I was shocked by my own profound grief, when I sent off the Surrender Application, so carefully prepared, after months of deliberation.

I had a client who left her marriage after 40 years. I asked her how she had done that — walk away from 40 years of a shared life of memories? "I focus on the time I have left, how I want to spend it. Sometimes you decide in the negative. I did not want to spend what I had left with him."

When my "surrender" was announced in the *Ontario Reports*, I wasn't given the option of paying for my own picture, as I had seen two retiring brothers do, some years earlier, smiling proudly as they closed the doors on their small-town practices. A lawyer colleague phoned me to tell me he had seen the words announcing my surrender in the *Ontario Reports*, and I learned of the announcement from him — no notice by the Law Society. Nothing personal. No notice at all. At least my surrender wasn't unique. It seemed there was a flood of these arising after the first wave of COVID. I wasn't alone.

In a daily meditation from Father Richard Rohr's Center for Action and Contemplation (November 19th, 2021, Week Forty-Six: Spirituality and Addiction), author and activist Holly

Whitaker speaks about the power of surrender as vital to the process of healing and recovery:

> I'd always considered the word surrender to be blasphemous. Surrender was never a possibility to consider; it wasn't something self-respecting, self-reliant folk like me do — we scheme around and bulldoze through whatever stands in our way. That all changed, abruptly, when I finally ran out of options and did the thing I thought I could never do — concede . . .
>
> The moment I finally let my knees hit the floor was when I finally stopped playing at life, and every bit of good that's come to me since then stems from this reversal of opinion on surrender.
>
> Surrender is the strongest, most subversive thing you can do in this world. It takes strength to admit you are weak, bravery to show you are vulnerable, courage to ask for help. It's also not a one-time gig; you don't just do it once and move on. It's a way of existing, a balancing act. For me, it looks like this: I pick up the baton and I run as far as I can, and I hand it over when I'm out of breath. Or actually maybe it's like: I'm running with the baton, but the

Universe is holding on to the other half of it, and we have an agreement that I'll figure out the parts I can and hand over the parts I can't.

Letting Go: Dad and the Keys to the Car

My father was about 85 years of age when I sold him my old BMW. I hadn't wanted to sell it to him at all. I had wanted to give it to him. My father wouldn't take it on that basis. So, I sold it to him for about half its then market value. A few months after our transaction, my father called me to complain that I wasn't cashing his cheques and this was disrupting his household budgeting.

Dad was 91 years old when he drove himself and my mother to the hospital, experiencing the first of several "mild" heart-attacks. My father's licence to drive was confiscated at this point. My brother-in-law drove the BMW back to my father's garage, where it sat for the next three years. He wasn't given any choice to take the driver's test again.

My son needed a car. He was in 2nd year at Queen's University. He had never owned a car, as it was against my principles to purchase one for him. He would respect the car and himself more if he purchased his first car on his own. I suggested he negotiate with his Papa John for my old BMW. My father was reluctant to sell the BMW. He thought the costs of repair to make it roadworthy would outstrip its value and that driving something that old could be a hazard to his cherished grandson. After some negotiation, he decided to charge $1,000, to make sure this would be fair to my sisters, and he told my son to give the cash to his Nanna. As my father signed over the ownership papers in the hospital, my son handed his Nanna the $1,000 in $20 bills, counting these out in a kind of ceremonial exchange. My father surrendered his car keys. It was the only time I ever saw my father tear up the whole time he was in hospital, wiping away the tears quickly with the back of a slightly trembling hand, those hands that had always been so steady, that had held a paint brush to letter the panels of trucks in the coldest of winters, or lay the finest brushstrokes to the bricks in an Italian piazza so that those bricks lifted from the flat surface of the canvas. He was letting go.

It would be months before he finally surrendered.

Dad was in his 94th year when he lost his balance on the small plastic stepping stool, caught the cupboard shelf and that shelf gave away. He fell to the ceramic tiles of the Woodbridge kitchen floor and broke his hip. "Just a step." The fall landed him in hospital, where he died some five months later.

Was it then, watching my father surrender his car keys when I began to appreciate that life is a series of surrenders — some seeming small, like the car keys, others huge, like life itself? Necessary surrenders. The way it is necessary for a snake to shed its skin in order to grow.

I have never been able to let go of anything easily, not even the pain. Maybe especially the pain. Do any of us? Feeling means we're alive. It is the reason my father refused opiates in the end. He wanted to feel, to be aware. To know that he was still human. Still alive.

I am struggling to let go of this collection, *Winners and Losers*. I have been over each story, the configuration of stories, whether to leave this in, take that out, innumerable times. To help me with the letting go, preparedness for what will come, I stand in QiGong Wu Ji posture — QiGong being a new practice for me, although very ancient. Wu Ji — the highest state of nothing, the beginning of everything, says my new QiGong instructor.

And now my heart tells me it is time to let it

go and send *Winners and Losers* to the publisher. There are so many I need to thank, all those hike instructors who guided me up my many mountains, the senior silks who tugged on my gowns and told me when to sit down, the young women who stood alongside me, at law school, and out into the practice of law and were my mentors, who taught me that on the other side of fear lies freedom. Mostly, they taught me that it is possible to have your cake and eat it too, to be able to work and have children and run households and law practices—albeit at great cost and sacrifice, embracing all that nourishes a full life. I also give thanks to former clients who entrusted me with their lives and often became friends and with whom I have continued the conversation. I feel I learned far more from you than you ever learned from me.

In his Epilogue to *The Splendid and the Vile*, Erik Larson quotes Pamela Churchill, writing a letter, on April 1, 1945: "Supposing the war ends in the next four or five weeks. The thought of it sort of scares me. It is something one has looked forward to for so long that when it happens, I know I am going to be frightened. Do you know at all what I mean? My adult life has been all war, and I know how to grapple with that. But I am afraid of not knowing what to do with life in peace-time. It scares me horribly. It's silly, isn't it?"

No, Pamela, I don't think it's silly. Most of us spend most of our working lives, waiting for the weekends, wishing we could be free of our work, particularly if we have had any ambivalence about our jobs or vocations. Few of us spend any real time being grateful to have a useful occupation, spend any real time planning for retirement. I have spent all of my time in retirement in the grips of the COVID pandemic, as my neigh-bours and I, my community, city, province and country grapple with how to cope, how to work, how to find purpose, how all of this fits in the global community, let alone functions in the universe. I am afraid of not knowing what to do with what is left of my life once the fear of pandemic is over. Is it a fear of death, or a fear of living? How to make every part of this precious life, whatever the challenges — purposeful and pro-ductive? How to give back? Is it even possible that to give back I must learn to surrender?

Taking off the robe, I'm surrendering the cover. It is my choice. I'm dropping the curtain. I'm down to me naked. Who am I, today, without the vestments?

If I am able to do this, surrender now what may be a final manuscript, it is because I know I am at the beginning of another publishing process that will see me climbing a mountain again. It will be a similar publishing process to the ones that preceded it, although every mountain is different and somehow the same; every mountain takes practice and perseverance. There will be the final edits, which always feel like a second chance, though publishers hate writers to make any changes at a late stage just before publication, discussions over cover artwork and print design. There will be the next book. My father always said of his artwork—"The best is yet to be ..." But this work. This time. It is as if I know there will only ever be one *Winners and Losers*. My last chance to get it right. To express all the love, ambivalence, conflict, and tenderness that I feel for this profession and for the work that sustained me over four decades, that supported the roof over my head and that of my son, and for which I am supremely grateful. The vocation of law. I always doubted I truly had that vocation, that calling, always felt, somehow, like a fraud. With practice, the practice must have grown on me. How did I not realize?

What? Over so soon? I used to joke with my clients that childbirth and death were the only realities that could not be adjourned. As a litigator, I had always been able to negotiate an adjournment. It was just a matter of price.

Surrendering this work is a letting go of another part of myself, another falling to my knees. I know, in my heart of hearts, that without surrendering, I cannot get up again. I cannot begin again that slow climb back up another mountain.

So, for now, anyway, I put down my pen. So, for now, anyway, I press SEND. In faith that I am not alone. What is that I feel tugging gently at the other end of my baton, like a baby's hand clasped around my index finger? I'm feeling a little breathless right now. Maybe I'll call it a night. For now, anyway ...

Acknowledgements

"*Château Cuisine*" was originally published as "Château Stories" in *Stations of the Heart*, Exile Editions, ISBN 978-1-55096-262-8, © Darlene Madott, 2012.

"First Gifts" in "Pasta With The Priests" was originally performed in 2008 by the Junior Choir of St. Michael's Choir School, commissioned in memory of Kathleen Mann (1919-2007). From 1939 until her retirement in 1984, Miss Mann taught every choir boy at the school as the Grade 6 teacher, including Marcus Madott Henderson. The music for "First Gifts" was composed by alumnus Kola Owolabi with lyrics by author Darlene Madott.

"My House of Many Rooms" was originally published in *Unbraiding the Short Story*, ed. Maurice A. Lee, for the 13th Bi-Annual International

"Winners and Losers" was short-listed for the Carter V. Cooper literary award, 2017, and was originally published in the *Carter V. Cooper Short Fiction Anthology — Book Seven*, © Darlene Madott and Exile Editions, 2017, and *ELQ (Exile: the Literary Quarterly) Magazine*, Vol. 42, No. 2, 2019.

Human Acknowledgements:

Francine Madott Kresnik, sister in sorrow, if only we could find that lake again in which to paddle like children together.

John and Francesca, for your first gift: that I was born of your love and have lived all my life in the knowledge of your love for each other and for me.

Marcus, you were intended, conceived by two persons who loved each other at the time. Thank you for being you. If I have accomplished anything in this life, it is because of the love of you.

Maria Costa, would the gentle voice in my ear be yours in my final hours.

John Razulis, first reader, spiritual guide and friend for many decades, with thanks for always reminding me to love with my whole heart, whole mind, whole soul and whole strength.

Mary Walkin Keane, for all the years of listening to my yearning, and for listening, listening.

Gina Bertolin, for an unexpected friendship at a necessary time.

Patti Latyshko, for giving me your trust, friendship, and story.

For all who have loved me and not loved me, just the same, God's grace and forgiveness.

For all I have loved and not loved, just the same, God's grace and forgiveness.

Land Acknowledgement:

I acknowledge I live on borrowed land, where this work was created, near the Humber River, for thousands of years home to Indigenous Peoples, including the Mississaugas, the Anishinaabeg, the Chippewa, the Haudenosaunee, the Wendat, many diverse First Nations, Inuit, and Metis peoples. "This House of Many Rooms" was written near the Shared Path (*Maada-oonidiwinan Mikaansan, Hachette, Dedwata 'se'*), which I walk daily.

I also acknowledge that my birthplace, Toronto, is covered by Treaty 13 signed with the Mississaugas of the Credit, and the Williams Treaties signed with multiple Mississaugas and Chippewa bands. I would not be here but for my grandparents who emigrated to Toronto from Calabria and Sicily in Italy in the early 1900s, and settled here. Toronto is where my parents met, married and shared paths. Their love led to me. I am grateful for those before, now and after, who share paths.

About the Author

Photo credit: Eric Fefferman

Darlene Madott has authored nine books, including *Dying Times, Stations of the Heart, Joy, Joy, Why Do I Sing?* and *Making Olives and Other Family Secrets*. She has twice won the Bressani Literary Award and has been shortlisted for the Gloria Vanderbilt sponsored Carter V. Cooper Short Fiction Award three times, as well as being a frequent finalist in *Accenti Magazine* competitions, among others. Her short fiction has been widely anthologized. A lawyer who practised for over three decades, *Dying Times*, her eighth book, grew out of aspects of her legal background and was a fictional exploration of the last journey. *Winners and Losers*, her ninth book, circles back to track the legal and life journeys through losses and victories from near the beginning. She lives in Toronto. For more about Darlene visit www.DarleneMadott.com.

Printed in December 2022
by Gauvin Press,
Gatineau, Québec